Her Two Cents

A NOVEL

J. Roylance Kraske

Copyright © 2012 by J. Roylance Kraske
All rights reserved.
ISBN-13: 9781495953712
ISBN-10: 1495953718

This novel is a work of fiction. Names, characters, places and incidents are the product of the author's imagination or are used fictitiously. Any resemblance to actual persons, living or dead, events, or locales is entirely coincidental.

For my Mr. Fribee. You are my heart.

Prologue

I rarely come home mid-week, but the academy administrators decided to try a new class format. So this week the schedule crammed my share of the teaching into two days and I finished up Tuesday afternoon. I like the new layout. The officers get introduced to more material by more instructors, I get paid for teaching the whole week, and I get two extra days with Libby. Not bad for a guy creeping up on middle age.

As I drive, my mind wanders around vague plans of what the two of us can do with the extra time together. I'm thinking three days at Lake Michigan would suit me. It's been a while since we made the drive since neither of us likes cold days on the beach. But I think it might be warm enough now that we can spend time beachcombing without worrying about our jackets. Libby's usually amenable to trips to the lake, so I think I'll have an easy sell on a weekend away. That is if she doesn't have a new batch of kids in dire straits.

I'm still daydreaming about beachcombing as I drive through Kingsford Grove and turn the last corner to the house. I'm surprised it isn't Libby's car in the driveway, but I recognize the one that's there at first glance. The dark blue Ford can be nothing but an unmarked cruiser. My mind immediately stops wandering and focuses on the Ford and the two men standing on my porch. I pull in behind the cruiser and turn the key. The radio clicks off and silence fills the car.

"Hey," I call as I get out. "What are you two doing here?"

I smile though it isn't something I want to do. Joe Waterford is new to the department and deserves my courtesy. Stan Farley is an old-timer and does not deserve anyone's kindness. I was partnered with Farley for a while and there's no love lost between us. Once his stint with Farley is over, this newbie is going to have to forget everything he's learned and start over. No one ever asked, but in my opinion new guys should never be partnered with Farley. He has his own way of doing things, and that way rarely follows the same rules that apply to the rest of us. Right now, I don't like it that the man is standing on my porch as if it's his own.

I get my bag and briefcase from the trunk and cross the gravel to them. I stop a few feet from the bottom step and wait.

"Where you been?" Farley asks. He makes no preamble to his demand. There is a pissed-off tone to his voice. I pick up on it even if he's said only three words.

"I teach, remember?" I reply neutrally, looking at him through my sunglasses. "These days I spend a lot of time at the academy. Just in case you've forgotten."

"For how long?" he asks.

"Why are you asking?" I ask in return. "You need my help to solve a crime?"

Waterford is looking uncomfortable. I feel for him. I was in his shoes often enough to know he can't do a thing about the way Stan Farley treats people. It doesn't matter if it's a witness, his partner, or a bad guy he was talking to. Farley is an ass. He's been an ass as long as I've known him. He'll never change, and I'll never let him off the hook. I may feel bad for Waterford, but I'm not going to do anything to help ease the tension. It's their call.

"We're looking for Elizabeth Lindt," Waterford says. "Do you know where she is?"

"Probably at work," I reply. "Why are you looking for her? You guys don't usually provide limo service for your advocates."

"Can we go inside?" Waterford asks with a sideways glance at Farley. "I think you'd rather your neighbors didn't hear what we have to say."

His ploy might have worked in another situation. But our house is on a huge corner lot and there's no way anyone could overhear what is being said unless they used surveillance gear. I knew if it had been just Waterford or if it had been Waterford and any other partner, I would have invited them in and maybe even made them coffee. But it's Farley. And there was no way I will let Farley in my house.

"Nope. As you can see, I just pulled in," I say, smiling at Waterford and ignoring Farley. "I'm not ready for company."

"Where is she?" Farley asks in a voice too angry for the question.

"Like I said, I just got home. She could be anywhere on a sunny day like this," I reply. I make a vague gesture to the sun and the blue sky.

"Yeah, you go ahead and be a comedian," Farley says. "We'll arrest you as easily as we'll arrest her when we find her. You may think being who you are will help, but this time you're going to find out that nothing can help you."

Hiding behind my sunglasses, I look from one man to the other. Something is not right. In fact, something is way off. Farley is truly a jerk, but something else is going on this time. Even he wouldn't come on like this unless something was in the wind.

"What's going on, Joe?" I ask. "Why are you looking for Libby?"

Waterford looks at Farley, who is staring daggers my way. I ignore him and wait for Waterford to reply.

"Joe?" I say keeping my voice calm.

The Art of Interrogation is one of the classes I love teaching. And I know I had been as good at interrogating suspects as I now was at teaching it to new officers. It was something Farley could never learn.

"What's going on?" I ask to prod him.

"We've got some missing kids," Waterford finally replies. "They were signed out from BB's on Sunday afternoon, and they haven't been back. Well, at least no one at the house claims to have seen them since then. Elizabeth signed them out. Said she was taking them to the park. We need to talk with her. We need to see if she knows where they are."

I blink. He said kids, plural. Libby dealt with kids every day. She checked kids in and out of The Bertram House on a regular basis. That was her life. I think she might love those kids more than she loves me. I wondered if the kids missing numbered three. I'd bet they did.

The Bertram Bernard House is part of the holding pattern for kids who end up in the legal system in Connor County. They either need to be taken away from their parents or don't have parents to begin with and need a place to stay. Libby was the last person I'd expect to take kids from the safety of that house. She'd worked hard to make it a contracted part of the county system. She served on its board and made sure the kids were treated with respect no matter what brought them there. Every year she helped raise the money that keeps it going. She put enough of her personal energy and money into it that I sometimes wondered if she was going to go broke in both arenas.

But I also knew that lately three of those kids and their situation had changed things for her.

"She took them," Farley says scornfully. "I know she took them. You know she took them. Where is she?"

I don't have the whole picture yet, but I'm starting to see where things were going. I haven't talked with Libby since I left for the academy Sunday morning. We'd shared an early breakfast, and I saw her through the kitchen window as I drove away. She could be anywhere. She could have done anything in the three days since I'd seen her. She could be helping that little boy and his sisters. But these two didn't need to know what I was thinking.

"Like I said, I've been at the academy," I reply. "I left Sunday morning and, as you saw, I just now pulled back into the driveway."

"We need to look inside," Waterford says, trying hard to stay calm next to his fuming partner.

"You know what I'm going to say," I say to Waterford. Farley's face gets redder because I'm so calm and matter of fact. Projecting calm even if you didn't feel it is another skill I teach new officers. "If you want inside you're going to have to show me a search warrant."

"We're not after you, Tanner," Waterford says, matching my calm.

I figure he's going to be good on the job. He learns fast. All he needs is a different partner. He needs a few months working with anyone but Farley, and I'm sure he'll do fine.

"The hell we're not," Farley's angry voice cuts the air. His face is too red and his breathing too heavy for a man who is doing nothing more than standing on my porch. "She took those kids and you know where they are. You're a guilty as she is."

"Do you have a warrant?" I ask. This time I look at Farley. I'm sure he sees his contorted face in my sunglasses and I like it.

"Not yet," he spats at me. "But we'll have one in no time."

"Then in no time you can come in my house," I reply, still calm. "But for now, I'm asking you to move yourself and your car off my property. No offense, Joe, but I think you need to be careful here. Whatever anybody else tells you, you need to follow the book. Make sure you follow the book every time you go out with this guy."

Joe steps down to the bottom step. Farley doesn't move. I wait on the gravel. I hold my suitcase in one hand, push my other hand deep into a pocket, and look up at them. They wait. I wait. Nothing happens. So I wait some more for them to get off my porch. I win the standoff.

"Come on, Stan," Waterford finally says. "Let's move the car and wait for the warrant."

Farley comes down the stairs slowly. I'm pretty sure he thinks he's giving me the evil eye as he comes toward me, but all he manages is a stare that doesn't amount to anything. He bumps my shoulder as he passes. I knew it was coming and braced myself. My body doesn't budge and Farley has to step around me.

Waterford pulls their car around the circular driveway and parks on the street in sight of the front door. They roll down the windows and settle in to wait.

I unlock the door and go in the house. The foyer at the bottom of the stairs is blissfully cool after the facedown in the sun. I leave the door open so they can see inside. Farley won't notice, but I think Waterford might include that note in his report. It might end up being important.

I turn on the answering machine as I walk through the living room to the kitchen. Nothing is out of place in either room and no messages play from the recorder. I get a beer from the fridge and walk into our bedroom. Nothing is out of place in here either. The room smells fresh. The bed is made up with my reading pillows right where they always are. No clothes are missing from the closet. No kids are hiding under the bed. And no Libby.

I change into shorts and a wife-beater t-shirt and check the room Libby made into an office. There's nothing new that I can see, and there's nothing out of place. I go and sit on the top step of the porch. I slowly sip my beer in the shade as I watch Waterford and Farley watch me from the car parked curbside while we all wait for the warrant to arrive.

What have you done, Libby? I think. *What the hell have you done?*

Part 1

I wasn't happy that I couldn't move on to my assignment at the police academy until we cleared our files. The "we" I was dealing with was me and Stan Farley.

In my twenty-two years on the Kingsford Grove police force, I'd had four partners. I'd been partnered with each of the other three for more than six years and partnered with Farley for an unlucky thirteen months. The current stint had turned out to be the hardest.

Farley was not the kind of guy I wanted with me in a sticky situation. I'd be doing things by the department rulebook, and the only thinking he was doing was whether or not I was following his personal rules. I'd be doing my best to keep the lid on things, and he'd step in with his face red and his voice ugly and mean. Situations always went from bad to worse when Farley was around. He was a hardheaded ego walking around in a suit. He filtered everything we did though rules no one else knew about. His rules seemed designed to make him look good in his own head.

I was pretty sure he didn't live in the real world. And I was pretty sure we'd been assigned as partners because the chief thought maybe I could teach him some of the stuff I'd be teaching at the academy.

For the last four years, I'd been given temporary assignments with several new cops who'd been reported as over-zealous or abusive with their interrogations techniques. My specific orders from Lt. Bradshaw were to make sure those guys knew the department rulebook and had a few new skills to keep them from repeating their bad performances.

Although Lt. Bradshaw didn't give me orders about Stan Farley, I guessed they were the same. Farley wasn't new to the job, but maybe he needed new skills.

As a rule I didn't talk with the old partners of my new ones. I like to form my own opinions, make my own observations. But this time I made an exception. I'd noticed how Farley had been floating among the departments for a few years. This was unusual, and I wanted to know what was going on with him. What I really needed to know was how important it was for me to carry the load and cover my back.

Every one of his old partners hesitated when I asked about him. Usually one cop is careful not to badmouth another. But after that first hesitation, they opened up. *"He's an asshole"* was the most common answer I got to my questions. *"Watch your back"* was the second. After that there were lots of quiet mumbles about the things he'd done and the fallout that resulted from his egotistical judgment.

A year later, he still hadn't learned a single thing from me. And I agreed with every word his other partners said about him.

The last case we needed to close before I got to move on was a series of convenience store robberies. Four stores on the west side of town had been hit in twelve days. It shouldn't have been tough to find our guy. He showed up on all the store cameras, so we knew he wasn't a pro since he didn't case the stores before the robberies. I'd been doing this long enough that I could tell our guy was actually a kid. Not only was he small and wiry on the videos but he picked at his face while he waited for the clerks to bag the money. Disgusting as that was, I guessed he was picking at teenage acne. A bad complexion fit with the oversized jeans and flannel shirt he was wearing in two of the videos.

But we'd had no luck finding him. None of the clerks found him in the mug books, which wasn't a surprise if he was new to the game.

And there seemed to be no pattern to how he picked the stores. One of the robberies was a 7-Eleven and the others were little Mom-and-Pop stores catering to their neighborhoods. They had different hours and different security systems.

The clerks said he came up to the register with packaged lunchmeat, loaves of bread, milk, and peanut butter and jelly. They rang up the purchase, and, as soon as the drawer popped open, he pointed a gun at them through his coat pocket and told them to put the cash in the bag with the food. No one had seen the gun, but each of them was sure he had one in his pocket.

The robberies were three days apart and happened just as most folk were sitting down to dinner. The spacing of the crimes and the food he took seemed to be the only common denominators. None of what we knew was very helpful.

We'd already put in a full day. I thought Farley had gone home when I decided to do some after-hours work on my own. I gave this kid some thought and drove around the neighborhood where he'd done the robberies. I went into one of the stores he'd robbed and bought a couple cans of iced tea and a box of crackers. When I got back to my car, I spread a city map on the passenger seat and anchored it down with the cans. I don't know why, but I figured the next store he'd hit would be close to the last one. I drew a circle around the two most recent robberies, picked a street in between them, and parked to wait.

I knew I should call Farley. Partners are supposed to keep each other informed. They're supposed to work together. But it had already been a long day with him, and I couldn't bear his company for another minute. So I didn't say anything to him or anyone else about what I was doing. I just parked my car and waited.

Sure enough, a call came through of a robbery in progress not three blocks from where I was sipping my first cold can of tea. I drove to the store, parked at the curb, and took a quick look inside the store windows before pressing my back against the wall next to the door. For a minute, I concentrated on the noise inside. I heard the cash register's *ting* and the drawer slide open. I listened harder but there was nothing more.

Before I expected it, the kid came barreling out the door still looking behind him. I put out a leg, he stumbled over it, and I put my foot in the middle of his back when he hit the sidewalk. Milk soaked into the money that fell out of the bag onto the sidewalk.

I had him in cuffs when a black-and-white showed up. I turned the whole thing over to them and went home for supper. The clerk would be interviewed. The kid would be processed. The counselors at The Bertram House would be called so someone could come and get him if they had an empty bed. We'd start the interrogation in the morning after a public defender and a child advocate showed up. He'd be fine until then. I didn't give him another thought all evening.

But I should have gone back to the station with them. Things had changed for the worse when I got to there in the morning.

"Lt. Bradshaw wants to see you," the officer at the front desk told me when I came in the door. I groaned. I didn't have any idea what he wanted me for but a summons to his office was never good.

Lieutenant Bradshaw is a hefty man who stands less than six feet in his high-heeled cowboy boots. He often has to look up at the men he commands, but there is no doubt that he has our respect. With the exception of Farley, Lt. Bradshaw has been able to either move on or move out most of the deadwood in our division. His hair is graying at the temples, and his big palms often go to his head in a nervous gesture that suggests his can't get used to the new color. His suit is always blue and his tie always a diagonal stripe of some sort except during December. During December he wears ties with all sorts of holiday designs. The ugliest one I'd seen him wear had Santa and eight reindeer with a bright blinking light for Rudolph's nose. Right behind that is a Grinch tie he got from one of his grandsons. It has a huge green head, big bug eyes, and a leering grin that gives me the creeps every time I see it.

I dropped my briefcase on my desk as I passed, walked to the back of the room, and tapped on the window in his office door. His gruff voice called me in.

His desk was piled with the usual reports and computer printouts. Awards were displayed on the wall behind him along with lots of pictures of him with his family and important people from the city. In spite of what some of the guys called his ego wall, he is one of the good guys. He treats us like we're human beings.

"You wanted to see me?" I asked.

He was standing behind his desk. In front of it was a small woman with wild hair twisted into a knot at the back of her head and held in place by what looked like one of my mother's knitting needles. She wore mascara and maybe lipstick but no other makeup that I could see. I thought she was a looker in spite of the fact that her body was tense and the air in the room made me think she was about to explode. She turned and I saw clear, wide-set brown eyes. The anger in them caught me by surprise. I pulled the door closed behind me.

"He's not the one," she said tersely. Her left hand vaguely waved toward me.

"He's the one in charge of the robbery investigations," Lt. Bradshaw said. "He's the one who caught your kid last night."

"Maybe so," she said. She was still tense. Her shoulders were rigid and her fists clenched tightly together. "But he's not the one."

Lt. Bradshaw and I looked at each other. He already knew and now I knew we were about to deal with another Farley problem.

"What happened?" I asked. I wasn't sure if I was asking my boss or the little woman.

"Inappropriate behavior," she said. "VERY inappropriate behavior. You are not supposed to talk to these kids without a supervising adult in the room. I was in the observation room, not in the interrogation room with him. And, by the way, I just happened to stumble into the right place at the right time. Obviously, he was questioned before I got there. All I heard was the tail end of the intimidation."

I scratched my head. I could imagine what was said, but I knew I needed to play it cool. Lawsuits were always at the periphery of our lives.

"Sorry," I said. "What was said to who?"

"Sit," Lt. Bradshaw said to both of us as he sat down.

I moved to a chair in front of his desk and she took the other one facing Lt. Bradshaw's clutter. He'd had the foresight when he took over from our last boss to get comfortable chairs for his visitors. I guessed it sometimes helped in situations like this.

We sat in her glowering silence for a minute while Lt. Bradshaw thought about what to say. I looked at her. It wasn't the time for the thought, but I still thought it. She was one pretty woman. She was small, perky, and pretty. Her wild hair interested me. Now that I was closer to her, I was sure it was a knitting needle sticking out of her curls.

"Stan Farley was here when they brought the boy in last night," Lt. Bradshaw said to me. "He decided an interview right after a robbery would be a good way to get a confession."

"You can't do that," she said angrily.

Before she could go any further Lt. Bradshaw stopped her with a raised hand. I had to admire his control. He certainly had the skills for the hard job he was called on to do. Unless you knew him, you wouldn't know that the crease in his forehead was a barometer for anger. This morning the crease was the deepest I'd ever seen it.

"We *can* do that," he said. "But we can't do it the way it was done."

She calmed down a little when she realized he was agreeing with her. She closed her eyes for a minute. I watched her do some deep breathing and settle back in her chair. Even the knitting needle seemed to sag a little.

"What would you like us to do?" Lt. Bradshaw asked.

"Reprimand him," she said quickly. "And require him to make an apology to both me and Christopher."

"We can reprimand him," Lt. Bradshaw replied. "That will be in the works today. But I can't require him to apologize. That's actually in the union contract."

She looked back and forth between us. Her brown eyes were steely and the calm she'd gained with her deep breaths seemed to evaporate. We let the silence grow, but she was savvy to our trick. She waited and let the silence grow even heavier. Lt. Bradshaw didn't waiver, but I got uncomfortable.

"What if I apologize on Mr. Farley's behalf?" I finally asked. "I'm going to question the boy anyway. I could start by telling him that what happened yesterday was mistake."

She looked at me warily. Then she said, "Okay. I guess that would be good enough. My two cents' worth is that these kids have enough trouble in their lives that they don't need some bully calling them names. Thank you for trying to make things right. But remember I'll be in the room with him. Don't you dare try anything sneaky."

She stood and we followed suit. She held a hand out to Lt. Bradshaw. After a minute she held it out to me, too. It was small and soft and disappeared into mine. After gathering up the purse and bulging satchel that leaned against the leg of the desk, she walked purposefully out of the office and headed toward the hallway leading to the interrogation rooms. Lt. Bradshaw and I sat down when she was gone, both of us letting out long sighs.

"Who was that?" I asked.

"Elizabeth Lindt, social worker from The Bertram House," Lt. Bradshaw replied, looking down the hallway in the direction she'd gone. "She goes by Libby. I like her and I think she's good for us. She keeps us on our toes like nobody else from that place has ever done. This isn't the first time she's come in here to do battle with me. It's kind of fun to watch her, isn't it."

"What happened last night?" I asked, ignoring his attempt to lighten the atmosphere.

"Patrol brought in the kid you caught," Lt. Bradshaw said with a sigh and a slow shake of his head. "They got him booked and put him in one of the cells downstairs. The front desk called the D.A. When the D.A. said to have the kid here at 10 a.m. today, they called BB's to see if they had an empty bed. Bertram's said they did and somebody would be here within the hour to escort him over. Before that happened, Farley got wind of things, went down to the cell, and bought the kid up to one of the interrogation rooms."

"Did he take anybody in there with him?" I asked. But I already knew the answer. Farley's rulebook said this behavior was okay.

"Nope," Lt. Bradshaw said. He held his open palm up to me like he'd held it up to Elizabeth Lindt. "I know Stan went completely against the rules. Ms. Lindt showed up, somebody went to the kid's cell to bring him up so she could sign him out and head back to BB's. He wasn't where he was supposed to be. The cell was empty. Then, instead of telling her to stay where she was while they looked for him, they told her to wait in an observation room. I'm not surprised about that. She's been around enough that the guys up front know her. She picked a room, walked in to wait, and saw the kid in the interrogation room with Farley."

"What are the chances?" I asked.

"Thirty-three point three," Lt. Bradshaw said with a grimace. "We only have three interrogation rooms."

I snorted softly and shook my head.

We sat without talking for a couple of minutes. I don't know what Lt. Bradshaw was thinking about, but I was thinking about that knitting needle. It was dark red with a silver top and skinnier than the ones I remembered my mother using. I wondered how Ms. Lindt put it in her hair and whether or not it hurt when she did. And I was thinking about how that little hand had felt in mine when I shook it.

"What did he say to the boy?" I finally asked. I didn't really want to know. Farley was always saying things that nobody wanted to hear. But I thought I should know what I'd be apologizing for.

"Libby said the kid was cowering in a corner with Farley over him," Lt. Bradshaw replied. "We don't know how he got on the floor. And we don't know exactly what Farley said to him. All she heard when she opened the door was Farley calling him a scrawny, pimply faced weasel. But the situation was pretty bad. It was probably a good thing she showed up. Who knows what Farley might have done if she hadn't interrupted."

Farley's words fit the kid. He was scrawny. And my guess about why he picked at his face on the store videos was right. He had a bad case of acne. Still, none of us got to play bad cop without a good cop around to keep us honest. Farley probably hadn't done too much wrong this time, but he'd been caught at it.

"He'll be on leave?" I asked.

"I'm working on six weeks' unpaid starting as soon as I can get the paperwork though channels," Lt. Bradshaw nodded. "I want you to go talk with the boy, Tanner. You finish this one up and get me the report. Then you've got a week to shift gears before you grace the academy with your presence."

I nodded and stood up. I was all but out of here. Farley was going to be someone else's problem. I was very grateful for that.

When the call came in, Libby was working in the small conference room beside another advocate, two volunteers, and a teenaged girl with a large silver stud in her right nostril. Libby and a volunteer pulled labels from sheets, lined them up on envelopes, and smoothed them into place. The girl took an envelope and added a stamp in the upper right-hand corner. The others folded letters and put them in the prepared envelopes.

They had over eight hundred solicitations to get ready for Friday's mail. After this one was sent, a smaller mailing would be put together inviting select community members to support The Bertram House by sponsoring tables at a Spring Fling Breakfast. The food for the fundraiser was being donated by local grocery stores, cooked by firefighters, and served by center staff and residents.

A short woman in jeans interrupted their chatter when she poked her head into the room.

"You've got a call, Libby," she said.

"Be right there," Libby replied.

"We'll finish up," one of the volunteers said. "Go home after the call."

"Thanks," Libby said. She smiled to herself as she walked down the hall to the office she shared with four other people.

When she was young, Elizabeth Lindt had no plans to be a social worker. She certainly never planned to deal with kids in trouble. In her young dreams, she was the woman behind the charismatic man who won all his court cases. She was the go-to person the rest of the office sought out when they needed some obscure ruling to win a case.

Libby's smile was a bit rueful at how things had turned out. She still thought she would have been a great legal aid and sometimes regretted her choice a little. But the smile also held a lot of happiness that she was helping so many kids. She had turned a knack with kids into a job that paid her well. And she knew she was good at what she did. She knew the lawyers and judges she worked with respected her. She even had the trust of the cops.

She found a yellow tablet and pen before picking up the phone receiver and sitting at her assigned desk by the window.

"This is Libby Lindt," she said, lowering her voice to a professional level and holding the pen ready to take notes.

"Honey?" her mother asked.

"Hi, Mom," she said and laid the pen on the desk. "What's up?"

"I'm so glad you're there, Honey," her mother said in a rush. "I really need to tell you what Al's done to me."

"What's up?" Libby asked again as she squeezed her eyes shut and blew out a quiet breath. With the phone to her ear, she crossed the room and unlocked a file cabinet. She took her purse and a pair of athletic shoes from the bottom drawer and carried them back to the desk.

"How would you feel if I had black hair?" her mother asked.

"Black hair," Libby said. "Why do you ask?"

"I'll show him," her mother replied. "I'm going to grow my hair out. I'll let it grow to my shoulders, get a good blunt cut, and color it a nice black. I'll was thinking I'd look younger. And then he'll be sorry he said anything about my gray hair."

"I thought your natural color was sort of red," Libby said. She replaced her flats with the athletic shoes while she talked.

"Well, it was red," her mother said. "When I was young and you and your sister were little. Have you heard from her? Have you heard from Megan?"

"Nope," Libby replied. She rolled her eyes and looked at the ceiling. She said this every time she talked with her mother. "I haven't heard from her. My two cents' worth is that I'm not going to hear from her. Mom, why are you thinking about your hair?"

"My current husband said my tangerine dress doesn't look good with gray hair," her mother replied angrily. "As if he knows anything about style. I like that dress and I'm not getting rid of it."

"And you're going to cut and dye your hair so you can wear an orange dress," Libby said. "What exactly did Al say?"

"He said the dress was meant for someone younger," her mother replied angrily. "And the dress isn't orange, Honey. It's tangerine. Didn't you listen to me?"

"What kind of dress is it?" Libby asked, ignoring the jab. She leaned back in the chair and looked out the window.

"It's wonderful, Honey," her mother crooned. "It's this chiffony thing with no sleeves and a jeweled belt and a long skirt. I look wonderful in it. Think senior prom and you'll know what I mean."

"Maybe Al didn't mean that anything is wrong with your gray hair," Libby said. She closed her eyes and shook her head. Everything was always about Diana. To her mother, nothing existed except how it related to her. Things hadn't changed since Libby was a kid.

"Remember you were telling me about your upper arms and the way they embarrass you because they jiggle?" she continued. "Maybe that's what he means. Maybe you need a dress with sleeves. Where are you planning to wear it?"

"Well, I don't know exactly," her mother replied. "He takes me to dinner every other Thursday. I thought I'd wear it the next time we go out."

"Do you go someplace where you can dance?" Libby asked. "It sounds like you bought a dancing dress."

"No, we don't go dancing," her mother snapped back. "He just takes me to dinner. I pick a different restaurant each time. Sometimes there's a movie we want to see. But usually we just eat and come home."

"My two cents' worth is that the dress sounds pretty fancy to wear to a restaurant and a movie theater," Libby said. She knew her mother would think she was picking a fight. "Even a restaurant and movie theater in Boston. Maybe you should return the dress and find a pantsuit you like. You love pantsuits, Mom. Maybe you can find one in tangerine. If you got something like that you wouldn't need to dye your hair."

"Did he call you," her mother asked angrily.

"Who?" Libby asked. She'd long ago learned to not react to her mother's anger.

"My current husband," her mother sighed. "That's exactly what he wants me to do."

"Al didn't call me. Al wouldn't do that," Libby said. She took a deep breath and flexed her back to relax. "I think Al likes your gray hair, Mom. You had gray hair when he married you. I think he wants you just the way you are."

The phone was silent. Libby waited.

"Mom?" she finally asked.

"Well, Honey," her mother whined. "I really like the dress."

The line was silent and Libby let the conversation stop.

"But I'll think about returning it," her mother sigh. "I guess he'd like that."

"Okay," Libby said slowly, making each letter a syllable. "Let me know what you decide."

"I will," her mother replied. "And you let me know if you hear from Megan, okay"

Libby put the receiver it its cradle. She looked at the ceiling and then out the window again. She would never figure her mother out. Megan had been gone for twenty years. Her mother knew that. But ever since Libby left home, the question came up in every one of their conversations. It didn't matter if they talked twice in a week or not for a month. Diana made sure to ask about Megan. Why did she always ask if Libby had heard from her? Why didn't she accept that Meg was dead?

Libby was tired of repeating the same conversation over and over. She wished her grandmother was still alive. She needed her guidance. She thought it might be time to call one of her uncles again to get a new point of view. Her patience was wearing thin again. A call to Uncle Jarod would help bolster her resolve one more time.

As she stood up to leave, the phone rang again.

"Bertram House," she said in the low, professional voice. "This is Libby."

"Miss Lindt?" a man's voice asked.

"Yes," she replied.

"This is Officer Pitts with the Kingsford Grove Police," he said. "We just brought in a kid who seems to be homeless. I was told to see if you have a bed for him. You'll get the official call from the public defender's office tomorrow, but we were hoping he wouldn't need to stay here overnight."

"We have a bed for him," Libby replied. "I'll be there in about twenty minutes."

"Okay," Officer Pitts said. "I'm going off duty, but I'll leave a note that you're on your way. Just check in as you come in the door and they'll know what to do."

Libby took off her athletic shoes and put them back in the file drawer. A few minutes later, she waved to the overnight supervisor, walked to her car, and headed to the police station.

Elizabeth Lindt was waiting for me in the observation room when I went to look in on the boy and compose myself for his interview. She was standing with her arms folded across her chest as if she were holding herself together. I stood beside her and we looked in at him.

"Listen," she said to the window. "I've only talked with him twice. He hardly spoke to me when I drove him to Bertram's last night. He didn't say much this morning, either. But my antennae have gone up. Something is wrong. I need for to you try to find out what it is."

"What do you mean?" I asked.

She didn't look at me while she talked. She watched the boy through the window. Her face was intense, more concerned than I thought the situation warranted. The kid was bent over with his head on his folded arms resting on the table in front of him. We couldn't see his face, but I guessed his eyes were closed against the bleakness of the room and the situation he was in.

"It's hard to explain," she said, still looking through the window. "I've been doing this for a while, and I get the feeling he's hiding something. My two cent's worth is that his family's in trouble and he's trying to fix things for them."

"Like what?" I asked. My two cents' was that any kid who ended up here was hiding a thing or two.

"I don't have the foggiest idea," she said with a shrug. She turned to face me, arms still folded tight across her middle. "Just promise me you'll be kind to him. Whatever you need to do, be kind to him. I just feel something is really wrong."

"Okay," I said. "Is there anything in particular you want me to ask him?"

"He hasn't said a word about his family," Libby replied. "Will you try to find out something about them for me?"

"Sure," I replied. "I'll get him a Coke and then get started. Aren't you coming in? From what you said earlier, I thought it was pretty clear you wanted to be in the room for our conversation. Have you changed you mind about that?"

"No," she said quickly. "I haven't changed my mind, but I'll watch from here to begin with. The speakers are on so I can hear everything that's said."

"Okay," I said slowly. "But don't complain later that I didn't include you in the interview."

"I won't." She straightened to her full height and pointed a finger up at me. "And you be sure you don't try anything. I'll be in there in a flash if he needs me."

"I'm sure you will," I said.

I smiled at her and the knitting needle that seemed rearranged in her hair. I had no doubt about what she said. She would be in there if I made one wrong move or said one thing she thought was inappropriate. And I was sure that if the kid was treated badly a second time, there'd be more than a meeting in Lt. Bradshaw's office.

I put a buck in the pop machine for a Coke, poured myself a cup of coffee, and carried them to the interrogation room. I put the Coke on the table and took a chair across from him. The boy's acne was worse than I remembered from our brief encounter outside the store. It made him hard to look at. I took a sip of my coffee and set it on the table.

"Christopher, isn't it?" I asked.

He nodded but didn't look at me. I nudged the Coke toward him.

"If you're hungry, I can get you a sandwich," I said. "There's not a big choice in the break room, but the machines have two or three you can chose from."

He looked up at me then. His face was painfully thin. His cheekbones pushed against sunken skin and his eyebrow ridges looked like rough clay pinched into place. His pale skin was covered with painful looking white and red pimples that distracted from his beautiful eyes. His dark blonde hair hung in dirty clumps around his ears, and he impatiently pushed it behind them. He looked more exhausted than any teenager deserved to look.

"I could eat," he said. "How long am I going to be in here?"

"You know what," I said. "How about if we forget the sandwich? It's a little early, but I can order a pizza and it will be here in twenty minutes or so. There's a pizza place around the corner that we order from when we're working late. What kind do you like?"

His lashes blinked rapidly several times as he fought against tears. His eyes darted to the mirror and the door and back at me. He'd won the battle. He didn't cry.

"Sausage and mushroom?" He wasn't telling me. He was asking if it was okay.

"Be right back," I said.

I went to the front desk, gave the guy on duty my Visa card, and told him what I needed. On the way back, I poked my head in the observation room to check on Libby.

"What do you think?" I asked.

"The pizza's a nice touch," she said with a nod. "Thanks for that. My two cent's worth is still that he's scared of something."

I nodded. In the interrogation room, I saw that Christopher had opened his pop. It sat on the table while he paced along one wall of the room. I watched him for a minute without saying anything. His fingers dragged along the cinder blocks with their years of drab paint, then tapped into the corner as he turned around. His shoulders were as slumped as if he were a tired old man.

"I hear you had a run-in with my partner last night," I said, watching him pace the room. "I'm sorry about that. In my opinion, he had no business doing what he did. I apologize for his behavior. You weren't hurt, were you?"

He shook his head. Slowly, he came back to the table and sat down. He took a swallow of pop, looking at me over the can. I was amazed at his doe eyes, soft brown with long feminine lashes. They didn't belong in the haggard face. And the haggard face didn't belong on a kid that young.

"I've met other people like him," he said, shrugging his narrow shoulders in a sign of resignation. "I figure they're not really mad at me. They're mad at the world and they take it out on me because I'm small."

"That could be," I replied. I thought he was right on target about Farley and his attitude. His observation was that of a much older person, and I felt sorry for him all over again. "But just the same, I'm sorry you had to go through it. We'll keep him away from you from now on."

Christopher nodded.

"Thanks," he said.

"So how old are you?" I asked.

"Thirteen," he replied. "I'll be fourteen next month."

"And you've met a lot of angry people," I said. "Tell me about that."

He shrugged and fingered the pop can.

"Tell me about the robberies," I said. "You were doing pretty good there for a while. You pulled off four in a row without getting caught. I'm impressed."

He grinned. He played with the pop can for a minute, his eyes blinking rapidly. I thought he was going to lose the battle this time. I waited and let the silence grow.

"I had to do it," he suddenly blurted out. "I didn't know what else to do."

I nodded. I waited. He played with the can and tried not to cry.

"So you need some help," I said. "Tell me what you need, and I'll see what we can do."

"We were living in a car," he said softly. "Then one day my Mom leaves and doesn't come back. I waited as long as I could, but Molly got hungry and...."

He shrugged and scratched at his face. He turned scarlet from his shirt collar to his scalp and his eyes filled with tears. He gave up the fight and let them flow down his cheeks.

"Molly's your sister?" I asked.

He nodded.

"You stole food and money from the stores so you could feed your sister," I said it as a statement. I looked at the mirror and imagined Libby nodding at me with approval.

"Yeah," Christopher replied, looking at his hands. "I took the food so we could eat. But I knew I couldn't keep robbing stores without getting caught, so I got money for later when I had to buy stuff. I knew I'd only have one chance at each store."

"Where did you get the gun?" I asked.

"What gun?" he asked. His head jerked up and the brown eyes looked puzzled.

"The cashiers said you had a gun," I replied. "That's why they gave you the money. They thought you were going to shoot them."

"Oh," Christopher said sheepishly. I saw understanding come into his eyes. "I didn't have a gun."

He leaned back in his chair. He extended his index finger, put his hand in a jacket pocket, and pointed his "gun" at me through the fabric. I shook my head.

"Well, that explains why I couldn't find one outside the store after we arrested you," I said. "But the cashiers still thought you had a gun. That complicates things."

He watched me with tearful eyes and swallowed hard.

"I need to go and check on Molly," he said. "I left her in the car. I've been gone too long, and she might be wandering around looking for me. Maybe she got hungry and went to find something to eat."

He looked at me with those big brown eyes and I knew he was more afraid than he was letting on.

"We can do that," I said. "Where's the car?"

"I don't know exactly," he said. "It's around the corner from where you caught me. Then three blocks down in front of a store that's boarded up. It's an old Dodge. It used to be blue but it's pretty faded."

"How old is Molly?" I asked. "What does she look like?"

"She's five," he said. "And she's little for her age. She'll be wearing a red jacket. It's her favorite thing. If she's in the car, she'll be hiding under some old blankets on the back seat. It will look like a pile of rags, but it's Molly hiding under everything we own."

"I'm going to have one of the patrols go and find your car," I said. "They'll bring her here. Hold on."

I got up and went back to the front desk. I gave them the information I had on the car, the location, and the girl. I waited until I heard the call go out and then went back to the interrogation room. Libby had gotten two more Cokes from the machine and sat on the same side of the table as Christopher. She gave me a look that warned me to tread lightly.

"I'm going to leave you here with Ms. Lindt," I said. "The pizza should be here soon. And I'm pretty sure Molly will be, too. I'll be back."

I watched them for a minute from the observation room and then went to report to Lt. Bradshaw. He waved me in as soon as I knocked on his door.

"Well?' he said.

I told him the story and recommended that he talk with the powers that be to not have the kid charged. I figured once they knew the story, the store owners might be willing to go along with Christopher staying at The Bertram House and doing community service until the system could find homes for him and his sister. His problem with the gun was something I had no experience with. Somebody else would have to help him figure that one out.

I was back at the front desk to get the pizza when a black-and-white pulled up to the front door and an officer brought in a frail, dirty little girl with Christopher's brown eyes and long lashes. She was equally pale and gaunt. Her red jacket stopped just below her elbows and looked tight across the shoulders. She stood straight and defiant looking up and down the hall.

"Molly?" I asked. I didn't wait for an answer. "Christopher's down here. We've got pizza for lunch. Can you come with me?"

I nodded to the officer. She understood I'd take care of the paperwork later. Then I held a hand out to Molly. She stared at me for a minute, crossed her arms, and marched down the hall ahead of me.

She walked past the door to the interrogation room and gave me a suspicious look when I called her back. I opened the door and held it for her. She looked inside cautiously until she saw her brother. Then she flew across the room and into Christopher's arms. He didn't shake her off like most teenage boys would. He hugged her close and kissed the side of her head. I could see her crying silently into his neck. His eyes blinked furiously again as he struggled to be strong for his sister. I admired this sad boy with the sad complexion. He had the most courage I'd seen in anyone for quite a while.

There was a lot we needed to ask and sort out. We needed to find their mother. We needed to find out who they were and why they were living in a car. But I left them alone with Libby. They weren't going anywhere until they'd eaten and felt better. The D.A. would be here to do his thing and ask more questions. Then the kids would go to the safety of BB's until the next step of their journey though the legal system. Things could wait.

I was relieved that my last case was wrapping up. I wanted to move on to teaching. With the twenty plus years I already had and the five years I expected to teach at the academy, I'd be ready to retire before too much more time passed. I wanted to wrap up this last case and move on. Still, I figured the time needed to fill out one more report didn't make much difference.

Besides, I still needed to find out how that knitting needle worked in the head of curly hair framing Elizabeth's Lindt's pretty face.

Libby sat at the conference table and read the new three-fold. It briefly told the story of her home away from home.

The Bertram Bernard Home for Wayward Boys, now called The Bertram House and affectionately known as BB's, was established in the 1930's by a local eccentric who didn't trust banks. He hadn't lost a penny in the crash of 1929 and was bewildered by the suicides of several friends who had lost everything. He watched as their families fell apart, as his hometown began to disintegrate, and as homeless boys separated citizens from their money at a time when they had very little to spare.

Angry at the law's inability to control what he called the city's jackals, he used his money and intimidation to corral the boys, give them food and shelter in his large brick house, and organize them into work crews for the public good. At Bertram's direction and expense, they took care of city parks, repaired and painted houses, and even filled potholes. In exchange, he fed them, kept them clothed, and tried to educate them. If they refused to work or follow his house rules, he exported them to other towns.

The Home, as it was known then, employed a cook, a teacher, a housekeeper, two former police officers, and, when Bertram was too old to do it himself, a director who oversaw the details that kept the place running. He left his substantial wealth in a trust designed to pay the Home's expenses into perpetuity.

Libby read the brief history laid out in the brochure designed to coax money from local businesses. Time and inflation had changed things since Bertram's death in the 1960's. Forty-five years later,

Bertram Bernard's wealth still generated money. But it was no longer enough to cover all of The Home's expenses. It covered the director's pay, keep the big house warm, and feed fifteen kids two meals a day. It did not pay for the cook or the counselors or the rest of what was needed to keep the place running and take care of the kids

Bertram Bernard had no idea each child now welcomed into his big, old house would need lawyers and advocates. The world had changed around Bertram's House and his money couldn't keep pace with the changes.

The cook and the counselors were paid by grants that were reapplied for every few years with no assurance that they'd be funded. The clothes and books and tutors and everything else came from donations when these brochures touched someone enough to make them care about the plight of the kids. Most of the advocacy and the legal needs of the residents, now both boys and girls, came from volunteers.

Libby finished proofing the brochure and started on the letter that would be mailed with it. She jumped when the cell phone sitting on the table started to ring.

"This is Libby," she said.

"It's Susan," came the reply.

"Where are you?" Libby asked. "This meeting is going to start in about twenty minutes."

"I'm not going to make it," Susan replied. "Connie won't be there either. Our boss called a confab during lunch and we both need to be here. The good thing is that he's going to feed us."

"Okay," Libby said. "Is there anything you want me to tell the group?"

"No," Susan replied. "But take notes again, okay?"

"Sure," Libby said.

"Wait," Susan said. "I guess you could tell them we'll do a run-through of the new presentation at the next meeting and show them what we think can go on the web. Tell Sam we're getting close to something we like."

"Great," Libby said. "I knew you two would be good for this place."

"You really roped us in," Susan laughed. "We couldn't break up the Three Musketeers, could we?"

"Yeah, well…," Libby said. "I appreciate it."

"And we love a challenge," Susan said. "See ya."

Libby closed the phone and smiled. Her friends. Her long-time, childhood friends. Except for the two years she'd lived with her grandmother, from grade school through college, the three of them had been close. They'd gone their own ways after college not expecting to see much of each other. But they'd come back together with husbands and children and jobs and different lives. After all that, they were the Three Musketeers again.

She went back to proofing marketing materials until other people began arriving for the meeting.

Billy Temple and I have birthdays two days apart. I'm not sure if that's why we stayed friends for so long, but it might be the reason our friendship started.

My family's birthday tradition is a cake with candles, including an extra candle for us to grow on, and whatever the birthday kid wants for supper. I love my mother's baked beans and wieners, and I've chosen it as my birthday dinner for as long as I can remember. I always ask for chocolate cake with raspberry filling and chocolate frosting with chocolate ice cream. My mother never fails to come through for me.

The year I turned six we spent my birthday afternoon at the park. Mom took my brother and sister and me to a spot under a huge shade tree, put the cooler on the table, spread a blanket on the grass, and turned us loose. I remember chasing Randy around the park for hours. We hid from our sister, Marta, pretended the drainage pipes were our fort, and made friends with other kids who were doing the same thing.

Mom lay on the blanket, read magazines, and napped while we raced around the park. Now and then, she'd call us back so she could count noses, but for most of the afternoon we were free from parental interference.

A couple of hours after we got there, another family claimed the table next to ours. Two girls spread their own blanket next to their mother's and sat down with paper dolls. At first, Marta sat on Mom's blanket and watched them. But when they offered her one of the paper dolls, she moved from our blanket to theirs and settled right in. Randy and I didn't have to keep an eye on her for the rest of the day. We shared a happy smile behind Mom's back before we saw the boy.

He stood in the shade watching the girls like he didn't know what to do. After a minute we grabbed him for a game of tag. Before we ran off, I noticed there was a cake in a big round plastic cover sitting on their table. It looked just like the one waiting for us at home. I knew my cake was in our kitchen, but this still looked suspicious to me. I grabbed Randy's arm and made him look at the cake. He just shrugged like he didn't know what my problem was.

"What's your name?" my brother asked when we finally stopped to catch our breath.

"Billy," the kid replied. "What's yours?"

He was my size. His thick head of hair was black and curly. Dad would have said he needed a haircut, but I liked the way it looked. It matched his eyes and made him seem happy.

"Randy," my brother replied and pointed at me. "He's Tanner."

"Who's the cake for?" I asked. "Is it somebody's birthday?"

"Mine," the boy said. "My birthday is Sunday, but we have to celebrate today. We don't celebrate things on Sunday."

"Why not?" Randy asked.

"That's the Lord's Day," he said. "We go to church."

"Oh," Randy and I said at the same time.

We ran across the park to the ball diamond where a group of big kids were playing kickball. Randall is two years older than me, and he walked right into the game and asked if he could play. Billy and I climbed up on the bleachers to watch and picked up the conversation where we'd left off.

"I'm going to be six," Billy said. "I start kindergarten at the end of the summer."

"Me, too," I said. I wasn't sure I liked that he was the same age as me and was going to start school with me in a few weeks. "It's my birthday and I get chocolate cake with chocolate frosting and chocolate ice cream. My Mom is taking me to school next week to meet my teacher."

Billy nodded.

"We just moved here," he said. "We used to live in a big house with my grandmother, but she died. Now we live in a little house. My sisters used to have their own rooms. Now they have to share." He grinned. "I still have my own room."

"Want to be friends?" I asked. I looked him over pretty carefully before I asked. So far, my brother had been my best friend, but he had friends besides me. I thought maybe I should have some besides him.

"Sure," Billy replied.

And just like that, we were friends. I remember his long, curly hair even though he started wearing a crew cut when we were in high school. I remember his intense dark eyes watching me in the park that day. It was like he was trying to figure out if I'd be a good friend while I was doing the same with him.

Through the years, we learned things about each other. In sixth grade, our teacher called roll using our full names. Billy was William Conrad Temple. I was Tanner Michael Moran. We didn't know that about each other. In seventh grade, we had to take choir. Billy could sing like an angel while I could hardly carry a tune. In ninth grade, we went out for track. Billy could gracefully vault over the highest pole. I was a runner.

His sisters were Abby and Erin, both younger than him. My sister Marta was the same age as Abby. Like us, the two of them became friends and I learned about the Temples from things Marta told me.

During the last weeks of our freshman year, we took aptitude tests to help us decide what careers we'd be good at. The results were supposed to help us start getting ready for college by taking the right classes in high school. It was no surprise to us that we both got results saying we'd be good at helping people. The guidance counselor suggested teaching or social work, but Billy and I decided we'd be firemen. And we decided that the one thing we could do that summer to work toward our goal was to take one of the CPR classes taught by the fire department.

It wasn't a bad plan, but it didn't happen.

That summer was the hottest one in ten years. Hardware stores sold out of fans. Some of the bigger houses sprouted air conditioners in their windows and on their roofs. Except for kids, the streets were empty from mid-morning until three or four in the afternoon. Adults stayed indoors whenever possible. Kids spent long hours at the city pool, the only place where we could stay halfway cooled off.

My birthday was on a Friday again that year. I'd gotten permission for Billy to spend the night and have my chosen dinner of beans and wieners with us. At lunch that day, in spite of the heat, my mother said she'd make him his own cake. I said it was okay with me, as long as he didn't get chocolate. She said we'd have a white cake and a chocolate cake and that I'd have to let him take some of each home for his sisters. My only question was whether or not we'd sing Happy Birthday twice. Mom resolved that by saying we'd sing once and Billy and I could insert the other's name when we got to that part.

I was happy. I was going to have two kinds of cake with two kinds of ice cream for my birthday. What more could a growing teenager ask for?

I rode my bike to the pool after lunch. I locked it up, paid my eighty cents to get in, and put my clothes in a locker. I spread my towel on the cement in the shade to stake out our territory. Then I jumped in the water and swam laps while I waited for Billy. Every day, he had to read to his sisters for half an hour after lunch, so he was usually late for whatever we did.

When he wasn't there by three o'clock, I moved my towel so he'd have trouble finding me when he finally came. I decided he was a jerk. I practiced diving, swam more laps, and horsed around with some other boys for a while. Billy had still not shown up when I left a little past five like I was supposed to.

The house smelled like brown sugar and bacon when I got home. Two cakes sat on the kitchen counter. Just like she always did, my mother had made me a round, three-layer chocolate cake with raspberry filling, chocolate frosting, and red sprinkles. The other cake was square, frosted in white with pale green frosting lines across the top and sides. I counted sixteen candles on each cake. I smiled to myself. I opened the fridge and saw two packages of Polish sausage on the shelf with the milk. A white mixing bowl covered with plastic wrap was filled with coleslaw. I smiled again. I had such a good mother. My birthday dinner was going to be a feast of my own design.

I rinsed my swimsuit in the kitchen sink, got a clothespin from the laundry room, and went outside to hang it on the clothesline. When I got back inside, my mother was on the phone.

"He's right here," she said. "Let me ask him."

She held the receiver against her thigh to muffle her voice.

"Was Billy with you at the pool?" she asked.

"No," I replied. "He didn't show up."

"No. He wasn't there today," she said into the phone.

She listened and I stood in the middle of the kitchen watching her. She squinted at the ceiling, making the furrows between her brows deep and dark. I started to go down the hall to my room, but she pointed a finger at me. I stopped and waited.

"When was the last time you saw Billy?" she asked when she hung up.

"Tuesday," I replied. "We stayed at the pool until the lifeguard chased us out. Billy said he was going to church."

"Do you know where he's been since then?" she asked.

"No," I said. "What's wrong? Who was that?"

"That was Mrs. Temple," she said slowly. "Billy hasn't been home since he left for the pool on Tuesday."

"Tuesday?" I asked stupidly. "He said he had to work with his Dad at the church on Wednesday so he couldn't swim. He said they had a church meeting last night."

"They didn't go to church last night," she told me. "The girls went to church, but Mr. and Mrs. Temple stayed home because Billy wasn't there. Mrs. Temple says they wanted to be home in case he came back."

"Then where is he?" I asked in a squeaky voice. I sounded stupid even to myself. "He's been gone three days."

"Mrs. Temple thought you might know where he is," Mom said. "Do you know where he's at? You're not protecting him, are you? I know you two are best friends, but even best friends shouldn't keep secrets at a time like this."

"No," I said, shaking my head slowly. "I haven't seen him since Tuesday. Honest, Mom. I don't know where he is."

"Okay," Mom said with a little smile. "I'm sure you don't but I had to ask."

She put her arms around me. I was taller than her and I leaned over to rest my head on her shoulder. Since we were little, she hugged us a lot. As Randy and I got older, we stopped hugging her back, but she understood. She still hugged us to show she loved us and whenever she thought we needed her support for something. She was careful not to embarrass us in front of our friends, but she didn't stop giving us hugs. I definitely needed one that day.

Her hug and the silence were interrupted by Marta stomping down the hall.

"Abby says Billy's missing," she said. "Do you know where he is?"

I straightened out of Mom's arms and turned to Marta.

"I've already asked him that," Mom said, her hand resting on my arm. "He doesn't know. And don't you worry about it."

"I bet you do," Marta accused me in a vinegar voice only she could come up with. "You have to tell them, Tanner. His parents are getting really worried. Make him tell, Mom."

"I don't know where he is," I said angrily. "I haven't seen him since Tuesday."

"Abby thinks you do," Marta shot back. "Everybody knows you two are best friends. Where are you hiding him?"

"Marta!" Mom said sharply. "If he says he doesn't know, then he doesn't know."

"We should organize a search party or something," Marta said sullenly. She smirked at me. "Lots of things could happen in three days."

"We are not going to talk about this right now," Mom said. "You both go to your rooms. We'll talk about it when your father gets home. Tanner, maybe you should try to think of any place he might go. Write down whatever comes to mind. I'm going to call Uncle Glenn to see if we should do anything. Go on. Both of you."

Marta and I exchanged a glance and then went down the hall to our rooms. She was right. Three days was a long time for Billy to be gone. I wondered why his parents hadn't called before now. I was sure Mom would have panicked the first night I didn't show up for supper. She and Dad would have called all my friends and Uncle Glenn that first night. I wondered if Billy had disappeared before and I hadn't known about it.

It was the only reason I could think of why his parents wouldn't have checked on him before now.

I stretched out on my bed with a tablet and pencil on my chest and thought about my friend, my best friend for almost ten years.

The only thing different about him was that he'd told me at the start of the summer to call him Bill. He was going to be sure the teachers and the other kids called him Bill when school started. I wrote that down on my paper.

I stared at the ceiling. The plaster was spread in big, swirling loops that almost looked like clouds. Off to the side above my bed was one small spot that was darker than the rest of the ceiling. I didn't remember the roof leaking, so I thought maybe rainwater came in under the shingles when the wind blew. The stain looked like a little bird with a long beak.

Billy was tired of going to church. That's what I'd tell my uncle if he asked. His father was some sort of a bigwig in their church and he wanted Billy to become one of his disciples or something. Billy didn't want to do that. He told me it was all a joke. He said all the going to church and praying was a joke. Mr. Temple had a girlfriend that his mother didn't know about. Billy was sure his father used the church meetings as his way to get out of the house to meet her without Mrs. Temple knowing what was going on. And it wasn't the first time.

Billy told me about other times when he was younger and he had to go to the church with his father. He'd wait in the chapel while his father met with the women he called his flock. The meetings would start with a group of women, the office door open to the hallway, voices in discussion floating out to him while he sat on a hard bench and did his homework.

Then, one by one, women would leave until just one was left alone with his father and the office door would close. Billy would finish his homework, read a book if he'd remembered to bring one, walk the hall away from the office if he didn't, and do anything else he could think of to stay busy. Once he even tried to sing every song in a hymnbook because the church was quiet for so long. Finally, the office door would open and the woman would walk out the front door. A few minutes later his father would come to find him

"Ready, William?" he always asked.

Billy would always nod. They'd drive home in silence, and Billy would sneak up the stairs to his room so his mother couldn't see his face. I wrote that on my paper. That's what I would tell my uncle if he asked me about Billy.

But the main thing I knew I'd have to tell was Billy's biggest secret. He'd probably stop being friends with me once he knew I'd told this one secret. When he turned fifteen, Mr. Temple said he would be old enough to train with him to have his own flock. We talked about this a lot because Billy wasn't sure what it meant. He was sure it had to do with the women his father met behind the closed office door.

I didn't say it out loud, but I thought his dad was planning to make Billy have sex with some of the women. It was the only training I could think of that had to do with the flock of women his dad said he was tending. We didn't know for sure this was the plan, but I thought it probably was. I was as curious as any teenage boy about sex, but I thought this was creepy.

Mom was calling Uncle Glenn because he was a cop. There would be no way for me not to talk to him. He had a way about him that made me want to be close to him, made me want to tell him what was going on in my life. He listened better than any other adult I knew. He'd gotten me to talk the time I had a fight at school and came home with bruises I wouldn't explain to Mom. He got Randy and me to confess to helping some other kids knock down Mrs. Carpenter's back fence after she yelled at them for no reason. And I knew he'd get me to talk about Billy.

I heard the doorbell, heard my mother answer it, and heard voices down the hall. My father's deep voice I recognized right away though I hadn't heard him come home. I thought Uncle Glenn was there. The third man's voice I couldn't place. I stayed on my bed listening to the rumble of voices, hoping no one would need to talk to me.

I jerked when my door opened. Marta slipped in and closed the door silently behind her.

"Where do you think he is?" she asked in a hushed voice.

All her anger was gone. I scooted over on my bed so she could sit down. The three of us kids had always been friends and we spent a lot of time with together until we turned into teenagers. Sometimes I was afraid of her and her vinegar voice.

"I don't know," I said. "What did Abby say?"

"Just that they thought he was over here," she replied. "He said he was going to have dinner with us for your birthday and then stay here until tomorrow afternoon. I told her that he lied to them."

"He said he was staying over here?" I asked. I sat up so I could look her in the eye.

"Yeah. That's what Abby said," she replied.

"Tanner?" my uncle said as he knocked on my door. Marta and I jumped.

"Yeah," I replied. "Come in."

Uncle Glenn opened the door and smiled at us. He came in, his big body making my room seem smaller than it was. His face was round and he wore narrow wire-framed glasses that kept slipping down his nose. His expression was as gentle as it always was. I couldn't tell how upset he was with me.

"How are you two doing?" he asked.

We nodded at him. Marta patted his arm as she crossed to the door, and then we were alone. He sat on the edge of my bed where Marta had been. He pushed his glasses up on his nose, leaned forward, and rested his elbows on his knees. I was familiar with this pose.

"Your Mom says you and Billy went swimming on Tuesday," Uncle Glenn said. "Is that right? That's the last time you saw him?"

"Yeah," I said. "He was late like he always is. So we stayed in the water until the lifeguard kicked us out."

"What time was that," he asked.

"About six, I think," I shrugged. "They come through the locker room to be sure everybody's out before they lock the doors at six-thirty. We were gone before they did that."

"Okay," he nodded. "Did Billy seem worried about anything?"

"He was the same as usual," I shrugged again.

"Do you have any idea where he might have gone when he left you?" Uncle Glenn asked. "Do you know if he left on his own?"

I must have looked startled because he put a hand on my knee and squeezed it.

"We have to think of everything, Tanner," he said gently. "I'm guessing he left on his own, but it's possible that someone took him. I know you two think you're grown up enough and big enough that no one could do that. But you're not. And Billy is smaller than you. Not much, but he is a little smaller. So someone could have taken him. Do you think that happened?"

"No," I said. "I think he's hiding someplace."

The words were out of my mouth before I knew the thought was in my head. Once they were out, though, I knew I was right. Uncle Glenn sat up straight and looked at me. *Tell me* his eyes said.

"He's pretty mad at his dad," I said softly. "Billy thinks his dad has a girlfriend again, and he's disgusted with him."

"A girlfriend?" Uncle Glenn asked.

So I told him the things I'd put on my list. Once I started talking, I remembered other things I hadn't thought of before. I didn't know where Billy was, but Uncle Glenn heard me out, listening to everything that poured from my mouth. When I stopped talking, he looked at me for a minute without saying anything. Then he looked at the floor and back at me again.

"What else?" he asked, pushing his glasses up on his nose.

I looked out the window and didn't say anything. I knew if I did, I was going to cry and I was too big to cry. Uncle Glenn squeezed my knee again. I looked back at those gentle eyes behind the wire-framed glasses, and it took me about two minutes to betray the friend I thought I cherished enough to keep any secret he told me.

"So what have you two been doing this summer," he asked when I ran out of steam.

I thought it was an odd question after everything I'd just told him.

"Nothing special," I shrugged. "We swim, we hang out. Nothing really."

"I need for you to think about the places you've gone since school got out," he said. "I'm betting he's someplace you went this summer. A place where he feels safe, a place where his old man wouldn't think of looking for him."

I thought about it. We'd spent a lot of time at the pool. We ran on the school track some evenings if it cooled down enough. We rode our bikes all over the place. We went to the library for the air conditioning on really hot days. Two or three times, I went with him to the houses where he mowed lawns. Almost every week, we went to his dad's church and he walked around and around it throwing rocks. He never broke anything even though he threw a lot of rocks and seemed to feel better for a while after he did. And we went to the campground on the river just outside of town. It was a long bike ride, but there was a lot of shade and we could sit in the water to cool off. We'd talked about asking our parents if we could spend a weekend out there camping, but we hadn't got around to that yet.

"Maybe two places," I finally said. "There's a house over on 8th Street where he mows the lawn. They have a big shed out back for their tools. There are a couple of lawn chairs in there. He could have slept in one of those, I guess."

Uncle Glenn nodded.

"Where else?" he asked.

"The campground," I said. "We rode our bikes out there a couple of times. It's nice, and there's a bathroom with a shower."

Uncle Glenn nodded. We sat quietly for a couple of minutes.

"Can you think of anything else?" he asked. He pushed his glasses up on his nose again. "Any silly thing you can think of might help us find him."

I shook my head.

"Okay," he said. "Mr. Temple is downstairs with your Mom and Dad. I want you to stay up here until we call you, okay? I'm going to send Mr. Temple home, and then you and I are going to take a drive out to the campground. That's my best bet where to look. I'll get your mother to fix him a plate of food and maybe cut him some of the birthday cakes."

I looked out the window as a car engine started up a few minutes later. Mr. Temple backed out the driveway and disappeared around the corner. Dad called down the hall to me. A few minutes later, Uncle Glenn and I were in his car headed to the campground. Two plates covered with tin foil sat on the back seat.

Lights pointing up from the ground spotlighted the campground sign. We drove down the narrow road looping through the campground and looked at the tents and R.V.'s. Only the three campsites nearest the entrance were empty. Uncle Glenn parked in the middle one, and we got out of the car.

"You want me to holler at him?" I asked.

"Why don't you just look around," Uncle Glenn said. "I'll wait here."

He sat on the hood of the car and propped his feet on the front bumper. I started walking toward the furthest picnic table I could see. It was already dark and I wasn't sure how we were going to find him if we didn't call out his name to let him know we were there. But before I made it halfway to the table, Billy materialized out of the trees.

"Who's that?" he demanded. "Why did you bring somebody here?"

"Why'd you lie and say you were at my house?" I demanded back.

"I'm not going with you," he said defiantly. "You can take whoever that is and go back where you came from. I didn't ask you to come."

"He's my uncle," I hissed at him. "My uncle the cop, remember? Your parents called the cops, Billy. They called the cops. Where did you think you were going, anyway? You're only fifteen. You'll get caught wherever you go."

"I was going to stay here for a while," he said. "I was going to stay here until I figured out what to do. I don't know where I'm going to go but it isn't home."

"Come on," I said and started for the car. "You can trust Uncle Glenn. You met him before. He's a good guy."

Billy hesitated for a minute, but then he followed me. We stopped a few feet from the car. Uncle Glenn got off the hood and reached out to Billy like he was going to shake his hand. Billy stood looking at him. Finally, he stepped closer and held out his hand. As soon as their fingers touched, Uncle Glenn pulled my friend to his chest and wrapped his arms around him.

"Tough week?" I heard him ask softly. Billy's shoulders started to heave though he stood pretty stiff and tried to pull away.

Over Billy's head, Uncle Glenn nodded to the car. I walked around them and got in, making sure to slam the door so Billy would know where I was. As I watched, Uncle Glenn asked questions and Billy answered them. Billy talked for a while, then Uncle Glenn, and then they were quiet. They stood like statues for a minute, looking at each other. It had gotten darker and darker under the trees, and I could hardly see them even though they were only a few feet in front of the car.

I had started thinking I'd made a mistake bringing my uncle out here when he once again put his arms around Billy. This time, Billy's arms went around Uncle Glenn and he patted my uncle's back. Then they were in the car and Billy was attacking the plates of food we'd brought. We drove to his house and I waited in the car while Uncle Glenn took Billy inside.

A few minutes later, Uncle Glenn drove me home to my own plate of food. Mom and Dad and Marta had already eaten and Uncle Glenn wanted to get home. The only cake missing was what we'd taken to Billy, so I took a big piece of each one. Nobody sang Happy Birthday to me that night, but it didn't matter. Billy was safe for now. Besides, I got two kinds of birthday cake with two kinds of ice cream. Mom didn't say a word when I filled my plate a third time.

I never knew what had happened to make Billy run away. He didn't explain. And he didn't tell me what my uncle did about it. But he did ease my conscious about what I'd done by saying *"Thanks, man"* the next time I saw him. And my uncle said he knew I'd understand that he couldn't talk about it. I was dying to know the details. Marta asked me over and over, but I had nothing to tell her that was worth passing on to Abby.

That night, out there in the dark of the campground watching my uncle, I changed my mind about what I wanted to do when I finally grew up. I'd be a cop. I'd be a cop, and I'd be as good a cop as he was. That night Uncle Glenn brought Billy back from something that could have become very dangerous. And he did it in a way that left my friend his dignity and our friendship intact. I wanted to do that.

Libby lifted the lid and poked a fork into the boiling noodles. She stirred, replaced the lid, and set the fork in the spoon holder. As they often did when she cooked, her thoughts strayed to her younger sister and the afternoon so long ago when she disappeared. Not really disappeared. Megan left with their father. And neither of them came back.

After all these years, Libby still could not forgive her parents for the selfish behavior that took her sister away from her. Wanting out of the marriage and divorcing each other was one thing. Using their children in the battle was another.

She had been old enough to understand some of what went on. Her father moved out after they had a big fight that included yelling and plate throwing. He mother wouldn't let the girls see him for weeks at a time. From the fragmented phone conversations she heard, Libby knew her mother wanted the girls with her and money to take care of them. Her father wanted the girls with him and his son-to-be ex-wife to take care of herself.

Neither parent seemed to give any thought to what was best for the girls. And neither parent ended up with what they wanted.

It was years after they disappeared before she had the thought that her father might have taken Megan because Meg was his wife's favorite. At other times, she was sure he just took the daughter who happened to be closest to the door. If Libby had been closer to him, Meg would be the one wondering where her sister was.

Either way, if he thought taking one of the girls and not letting his wife see her would lead to getting his demands, his plan didn't work. Her mother refused visits with Libby. In the divorce, she fought against giving him a share of the household belongings. Diana yelled her demands for money and support to keep the house into the phone night after night. Finally all contact between the two of them had to be through their lawyers.

Just before Meg disappeared they were making supper for their mother. Diana had gone to the beauty parlor for a haircut, and the girls decided to surprise her when she by fixing dinner before she got home. Libby opened a box and was melting Velveeta into elbow macaroni, and Megan was cutting tomato wedges for the salad when their father came in the back door.

"Hey, Babies," he said with his usual grin. "I see you're making dinner for Mom. Where'd she go?"

They nodded in unison as they stared at him. They held their breaths and didn't answer his question. He wasn't supposed to be in the house. Their mother had told them not to open the door if he knocked. But he hadn't knocked. They hadn't heard him until he spoke. It was like he appeared in the kitchen by magic.

"Well," he said as he reached for Meg. "Let's you and me go get her some flowers. That'll be a good surprise, don't you think. We'll be back before she gets home. You finish up our dinner, okay, Libby? We'll be back in a few minutes."

Meg's eyes begged her older sister for help. But their father's hand was on Meg's shoulder and there was nothing Libby could do. Neither of them could say no. Neither of them could challenge him.

And, just like that, her sister was gone.

Now, as Libby tossed vegetables into a skillet, she wondered again how long he'd been waiting for their mother to leave before coming into the house. She thought again that neither parent had gotten what they wanted. They got their divorce. But they each lost a daughter and their home. Instead of a severed marriage, there was a severed family and sisters whose last memory of each other was a sad one

That is, if Megan was still alive to remember that last day, she had to be as sad about it as Libby was. But Libby was sure her sister was dead. For years now, Meg had been old enough to walk away from whatever situation their father put her in. Libby was sure Meg was dead simply because she hadn't come back when she was old enough to do it.

Once out of her mother's house and making her own money, Libby hired a private investigator to look for her sister. But the trail was a dozen years' old. He had no luck and told her to not waste any more money. She took his advice and mentally declared her sister dead. In spite of that, she held a flicker of hope that Meg was alive. She couldn't help thinking of Meg and the years they'd missed.

Libby sometimes wondered how she could be gentle with her mother. She would never forgive her for losing her youngest daughter. And she couldn't quite forgive her for always asking about Megan every time they talked. After all the time that had passed, Libby couldn't believe her mother thought Megan was alive. She had to know Megan wouldn't be contacting either of them ever again. But still, probably because of her Grandmother and Uncles, Libby managed to handle her mother when she called.

As she turned down the burner under the vegetables and moved the pot of noodles to the counter, Libby shook away the old thoughts. Taking silverware from a drawer, she began setting the table.

Her small second floor apartment was cozy with mismatched furnishing she'd found at a used furniture store. An oversized green chair sitting beside an ottoman and a table cluttered with books and magazines announced itself as her favorite place in the room. A floral-print couch with fleece throw and several pillows invited afternoon naps.

The kitchen sported the once popular avocado green appliances. One wall was covered with pressed tin squares dabbed with paintto match the ugly green. The cupboards were an odd yellow that showed years of hard knocks from many tenants. The room was barely large enough for the tiny round table usually pushed against the wall.

She set the table for three then opened the fridge for iced tea. As she set a wooden salad bowl in the middle of the table, the doorbell rang.

"Hey," she said as she opened the door. "You made it."

"Right on time," a tall, thin woman replied. "Wait until you hear what we did."

Behind her, a shorter, rounder woman smiled as she took off her coat. Libby's mood lifted just seeing her fellow Musketeers. She banished the gloomy thoughts of Megan.

The two women were a Laurel and Hardy combination. Nearly six feet tall, Susan draped her thin body in bright skirts and blouses and wore bold jewelry. Connie was a half-foot shorter and wore unadorned blues and grays on her curvy body.

Both women worked in a public relations firm, Connie full-time as a graphic artist and Susan part-time in IT. Both were married with husbands and children. Both believed in Libby's crusade to help kids in trouble and she'd easily convinced them to volunteer at The Bertram House.

Dropping coats and purses on the couch, they made their way to the kitchen.

"We may have an answer to the finance questions," Connie said.

She put a white box on the counter, sat at the table, and nibbled a radish from the salad. Libby handed them iced tea.

"To friendship," Susan said and they clinked glasses.

"So tell me," Libby said as she poured the pasta into a colander. While it drained, she mixed olive oil and herbs into the vegetables. Then she tossed in the pasta.

"We were fabulous," Susan said, taking a seat at the table. "Absolutely fabulous."

"The Three Musketeers ride again," Connie agreed with a laugh.

"Come on!" Libby groaned. "Tell me what happened."

"I think we got a three-year grant that will pay for some of the repairs and for half of a counselor's salary," Susan said. "If we play our cards right and the city stays on good financial ground, we can probably get the grant for five years in the next cycle."

"Three years?" Libby asked. "That's great."

"I think Connie's CD showing the shelter and the kids is what did it," Susan continued as she filled her salad plate. "It just gets better and better."

"To say nothing of your narrative," Connie put in. *"Imagine sleeping on a thin cardboard mattress. You're fourteen. You've been kicked out of the house. You have no place to go.* She used Paul's story while the pictures played in the background. I tell you, Libby, before long we're going to be undefeatable. We are going to get every grant we apply for."

"She's right," Susan said. "We need a few more pictures of the streets where the kids end up when they run away or get kicked out. Then our presentation will be nearly perfect."

"We've decided we need *Before* and *After* pictures that the audience can immediately empathize with," Connie said. "*Before*: we show the streets, the cardboard mattresses, the dumpsters, and the other homeless people. *After*: we show The Bertram House with its clean beds and bathrooms."

"I'm thinking we need more shots of the kids in the rec room," Susan broke in. "Maybe we can add a few of them in their rooms studying. There might be security issues, but let's think about it."

"The other thing that might get us more, smaller donations is a list we hand out to the audience," Connie said. "You know what I mean."

"Right," Susan completed Connie's thought. "We can list the phone cards and bus coupons the kids always need. That way, everyone who attends will know that we need small things in addition to the grant to keep BB's running. Maybe members of the Elks and Eagles will make little donations once their organization dedicates big money to us."

"It's always a hard sell," Libby said. "Most people think Bertram's is part of the government. They don't understand we have a contract to provide housing for these kids. They think it's part of the police department and the jail. My two cents' worth is that half of what we do is educate the public about social services and what they are and are not doing. We have to sell our part in the picture. I can't believe you got money for three years. That's so great!"

They talked while they ate, cleared the table, and started making lists as they enjoyed the large brownies Connie brought for dessert. It was nearing ten o'clock when the two women left and Libby straightened the kitchen. She thought of her sister again as she wiped the counter. She wondered if Meg's life would have turned out as well as hers. She wondered if she was right to think her sister was dead. And then she tried to stop thinking about it.

In her bedroom, she got into flannel pants and a t-shirt. While she sat at a small desk to combine the lists they'd made, she jumped at a thumping sound. She opened the sliding door to the deck, leaned down, and stroked a soft, arched back near her leg.

"Well," she said. "Where have you been? I thought you'd found a new home. You haven't visited me in quite a while."

The big cat purred and rubbed against her leg.

"Come on," Libby said. "I bought you some tuna. I still don't know how you get up here, but I'll reward you just the same for coming to see me."

She thought the cat was beautiful. It was certainly unusual. Nearly as large as a lynx, he had a bobbed tail and pointed tufts of hair at the end of his ears. His gray-and-black tiger coat had one white paw and a white stripe down the nose. Blue-gray eyes often looked up from her lap as she ran a hand down whatever part of the cat's body it presented for stroking. Libby was sure he weighed nearly thirty pounds.

Months ago, she was curled up in bed with a book. She'd left the curtains open so she could see the city lights, and her heart rate increased when she heard a thump on the sliding glass doors. She looked up at the window but saw nothing on the deck. Her apartment was on the second floor and she thought no one would be able to come in the sliding doors. She convinced herself she'd imagined the sound and went back to her book.

When the thump came a second time, she cautiously walked to the doors and looked out. As she watched, a large gray cat lowered its head and thumped against the glass for a third time. She slid the door open. The cat came in, looked up at her with a meow, and headed to the open hallway door.

Libby had cautiously stepped onto the deck to look around. There were similar decks on each side of her, each with potted plants and deck chairs. But they were five or six feet from hers and had privacy latticework. All of the decks were too far from the ground for even a tall man on a ladder to reach. She couldn't imagine how the cat had gotten up there.

Once inside, the cat led her down the hallway to the kitchen like it knew where it was going. It sat in front of the refrigerator and meowed, looking up at her with mournful eyes. Libby cut up a chicken breast, stirred it into a little rice, and put the bowl on the floor. She filled a second dish with water and leaned against the counter to watch the graceful animal.

"So how did you get up here?" she asked when the cat finished the chicken and sat on her feet with its head tilted up at her. She got on her knees to pet the animal and found a brittle, yellow flea collar around its neck. No collar or tags, just an old flea collar. When she went back to her bedroom, she laid a towel on the floor near the sliding door. The cat curled in a tight ball on the towel and fell asleep. In the morning, Libby left the door open while she got ready for work. The cat left the way it had come while she was in the shower.

Now and then the cat butted its head against the sliding door and she let it in. Its arrival was unpredictable. Sometimes it came every evening for a week. Then it would not make an appearance for a month. By now it had graduated to sleeping on the foot of Libby's bed, and she found the heavy weight comforting.

When the cat finished its tuna, Libby lifted it to her arms and checked for a collar and any indication that it had been in a fight. Only once had she needed to clean a wound on the cat's side. Tonight the cat was collar and wound free.

"I wish I knew who you were," she said. "And I wish you'd stay a while."

The cat purred and rubbed its head against her neck.

After three weeks working with Stan Farley, I went to Lt. Bradshaw. Farley was tough to work with, but I'd worked with difficult partners before. It was more than that. I was sure he wasn't just difficult. Farley was dangerous.

"I know what you're going to say," Lt. Bradshaw said. I'd closed the door behind me and sat in one of his comfy chairs. He held up a hand to keep me from talking. "I'm sure you think he's a jerk."

I nodded and waited for him to say more.

"But we have to keep him," he continued.

"Why?" I asked. "We'd be better off with him at a desk someplace where he only talks to other cops. Can't you get him transferred to research or someplace like that?"

"You don't like him," Lt. Bradshaw said flatly. "None of his partners liked him. But he stays where he is. And I'm not going to tell you why. He's assigned to you because you've pulled more than one hot dog on the brink of destroying his career back to a path where he went on to be a good cop. That's all I'm asking you to do. Do what you can to pull Farley back from the brink."

This was the first time he'd confirmed out loud why Farley had been assigned to me.

"I can't do it," I replied and shrugged. "Nobody can do that. Farley will take direction from no one."

"Just try, okay?" Lt. Bradshaw sighed heavily. He looked tired as he stood up and dismissed me.

I hesitated for a minute and then I stood up, too. At my desk, I sorted message slips and decided none of them needed immediate attention. I opened one case file after the other, but I couldn't concentrate. Lt. Bradshaw's behavior had me wondering what was going on. Farley and I needed to do follow-up on at least three cases, but they all required going out into the field with him. I didn't feel up to the headache that came with being with him and other people.

Instead, I logged onto my computer and hit the Internet icon. Nothing came up when I typed in his name. I went to the local paper and typed his name again. Nothing came up except police department public relations stuff. I was rubbing my head and trying to think of some other way to find out why no one would deal with him, when the object of my contempt sat down across from me.

"You gonna sit in here all day?" he asked in a tone indicating his superiority and the fact that he resented me. He wanted to be the one to decide what we did and when we did it. "We have work to do outside."

"We do," I replied. On the slim chance that Farley might pick up on it, I thought I'd try modeling a politeness I didn't feel. "Which case do you think we should handle first? The home invasion or the break-in at the mall?"

"There's more to go on at the mall," he said. "Let's start there."

I nodded and picked up my coat. We were halfway across town when a call came through about a disturbance at a grocery store two blocks from where we were. I radioed that we'd take it, but to have back-up come as soon as they could. Dispatch told us they'd had calls from customers and the store manager. It was impossible to say what was going on, but people seemed to think that a woman was assaulting a little girl, probably her daughter.

Farley's face was pulsing red by the time he jerked the car to a stop close to the door, haphazardly blocking three disabled stalls.

"Keep your cool," I said as we got out of the car. "We don't know what's going on."

Farley nodded as he jerked his arms through the sleeves of his jacket. His face was still red and his eyes still narrowed. I saw trouble ahead no matter what I did.

"Stan," I said. "You need to calm down before we go in there."

I put a hand on his arm and he shook it off. I stepped between him and the door.

"Stan," I said again, raising my voice a little to be sure I had his attention. "Either cool it or stay in the car and let me handle this. We don't know what's going on in there, and we're not doing anything until we do."

He straightened his shoulders, took a deep breath, and nodded.

"I'm lead on this," I said as the electronic door whooshed open and let out cold air. "Don't do anything until we know what's going on."

Inside, a barrel-chested man stood beside one of the registers with two cashiers, a woman, and a little girl. The man walked toward us with his hand out.

"Dale Horton," he said as I took his hand. "Sorry for the call."

His nametag identified him as the store manager. I shook his hand, and the two of us moved to one side of the door as it whooshed shut. Before he could explain what happened, Farley was across the floor and in front of the woman. He grabbed her by the shoulders and started shaking.

"How do you like it?" he demanded. "How do you like it?"

The cashiers jumped away from him, taking the little girl with them. The girl started screaming as Farley continued to shake her mother. I took three long steps and grabbed Farley from behind. He was in a rage and I could barely hold on to him. I couldn't pull his hands off her shoulders or back him away. He kept shaking her and raging *Let's see how you like it* in her face.

Finally a customer helped me and the store manager get the woman away from Farley, and I backed him out the door. Our backup was jumping from their car as we came out. They looked confused when I pushed Stan into the back seat of their cruiser and closed the door when his feet hit the floor mat.

"Keep him out here," I said. "And don't let him out of your sight."

Inside the store, the woman was surrounded by customers, cashiers and the store manager. She held her sobbing daughter and rubbed her head over and over.

"It's okay, sweetie," she said. "Shh. Shh."

"I am so sorry," the store manager said as he led me away from them. "I should have checked to be sure what was going on before I called 911. It was really nothing. She was…well, the kid kept taking thing off the shelves and I guess her mother slapped her hands. The cashiers got complaints, they called upstairs, and I called 911. I should have come down to see what was going on before I did anything."

I sighed. The idea of one emergency number was such a good one. But it had evolved to a catchall for everything from real emergencies like drive-by shootings to the really-not-an-emergency like the infirm calling for help getting up from the toilet or a someone calling to complain that a car was parked in front of their house. With the increase in the number of people with cell phones, the number of false alarms every day was staggering.

"It's okay," I replied. "We had several calls from your customers so we would have been here whether you called or not."

I walked back to the group clustered around the crying kid. The cashiers backed away and went to their registers. The woman held her daughter on her hip and continued to gently rub the head resting on her shoulder.

"Are you all right?" I asked.

"Just scared," the woman nodded.

The little girl stopped crying and looked up at me from her mother's arms. I took a card from my wallet, turned it over, and wrote Lt. Bradshaw's name and number on the back. I handed it to her.

"This is our boss," I said. "If you want to file a complaint, call him to start the process. You can also go online to the police department web site and do it there, if that's easier for you."

She took the card and nodded. I nodded back, apologized again, and left the store with a wave at the manager.

What I wanted to say but didn't say, couldn't say, was that she should file the complaint. She should file it immediately and get every one of the people in the store to file complaints as well. If she didn't, there was nothing we could do about Farley. I didn't like the idea that she could sue the department and maybe get a huge settlement from the city. But Farley was way out of line and we needed complaints on record before there was any chance of getting him away from the public. I'd include his behavior in my report like I had before and file an internal complaint, but the brass hearing it from me wasn't the same as hearing from the public.

Outside, Farley and I got in our car, and I drove back to the station. Neither of us said a word the entire trip.

Rosemary Morgan stood on her front step and watched her daughter's car pull up to the house. Diana had not been home in years. Rosemary called her daughter occasionally, but Diana made it clear that the calls were not welcome. Now here was the eleven-year-old granddaughter Rosemary had seen maybe four times since her birth. She couldn't believe she had agreed to keep the girl for the summer while Diana sorted things out.

"Hi, Mom," Diana called as she got out of the car. She put her head back inside and scowled.

"Get out of the car, Libby," she hissed. "Don't you give me trouble today. I can't handle any trouble from you."

Libby glared back at her mother. She made no move to get out of the car. Diana grabbed her purse and glared at Libby again.

"Your Grandmother will have lunch waiting for us," Diana said in a syrupy voice." It might not be what you're used to, but she'll have something ready."

Libby looked straight ahead out the windsheild and didn't move. Diana straightened up and smiled at her mother as she moved to the back of the car. She unlocked the trunk and kept smiling as she walked to the house.

"Don't worry about her," Diana said with a wave of a hand toward Libby. "She's a little sulky today, but she'll get over it."

She stopped on the step and stood with Rosemary for a moment looking at the wild-haired child in the front seat of the car. Then she put her hands on her mother's shoulders and turned her around to the open door.

"I bet you have some of that Sun Tea waiting for us, don't you?" Diana said. Once she had her mother turned away from the car, she breezed past her and disappeared into the house.

Rosemary sighed. Instead of following Diana, she turned back to the car. Her granddaughter hadn't moved. Rosemary made her way down the steps. She walked with a painful gait to the trunk and lifted out a suitcase. Setting it on the ground, she took out a cardboard box, braced it on her hip, and closed the lid softly. She could see Libby watching her in the rearview mirror.

Rosemary lifted the suitcase and, with the box still braced against her side, she began hobbling toward the house. She moved slowly, protecting the hip her doctor had told her many times needed to be replaced with a new titanium version that should last her to the end of her life.

"Wait," Libby said loudly. She opened the car door, slammed it behind her, and hurried to her grandmother. "I can carry them."

"You take the box," Rosemary said. "I'll keep the suitcase."

"They're not heavy," Libby said.

As Libby fingered the suitcase away from Rosemary and took the box from her other hand, she saw her mother in a window drinking from a glass and watching them. She stomped up the steps and then waited for her grandmother to reach her before going inside.

Rosemary took a long time to get up the three steps. She rested her hand on Libby's shoulder as she passed and gave it a small squeeze, leaving behind a faint powdery smell. Libby followed her down the hall to a room with a twin bed, a table, and a dresser. Her grandmother turned and tried to smile at her as she looked around.

"This will be your room," Rosemary said. "Mine is across the hall. The bathroom is next to the kitchen. Put your things down. You can put them away later. I'm sure your mother has a glass of tea waiting for you."

The room filled with Rosemary's powder smell as Libby put the box on the table and lifted her suitcase onto the bed. She let out a sigh that nearly broke Rosemary's heart.

"Come on," she said. "Your mother wants to get back on the road, so I guess we better get lunch on the table."

Lunch was sandwiches and chips and raw vegetables that Libby dipped into a bowl of dressing in the middle of the table. The meal was eaten in an uncomfortable silence As soon as she finished her sandwich, Diana poured Libby a fresh glass of tea.

"This is Sun Tea," she said as she handed it to Libby. "You'll need to ask your Grandmother how she makes it. You might want to make it yourself when you're older. Right now, I want you to take this to your room and get settled. I'll say goodbye before I leave."

Libby took the tea down the hall. Setting it on the table next to the box she brought from the car, she crept back to the living room and sat down on the floor next to the couch so she was out of sight.

"I didn't do anything, Mother," she heard her mother say. Her tone was one Libby had heard many times. "He left. That's all. He left and he took Megan with him."

"Nothing is that simple," Rosemary replied. "I don't need to know what happened between the two of you. I don't need to know, but I do think you should tell Libby."

"I don't need to explain anything to Libby," Diana huffed. "She was there, Mom. She knows exactly what happened. And I don't need you telling me what to do with my own daughter."

The room was quiet for a minute and Libby thought she should sneak away to her room.

Then her mother asked in a too-happy voice, "When did you move in here"

"You're changing the subject," Rosemary replied. "If you need to know, Dr. Reynolds recommended I downsize because of my hip. He says it needs to be replaced."

Diana said nothing and she didn't look at her mother.

"I'm putting the operation off as long as possible," Rosemary told her. "The farm is leased and they're living in the old house. I'm here with no stairs, a lot less house to take care of, and all the vegetables I can pick from their fields."

"What a switch," Diana said. "Dad's helper and his wife living in his house and you living here."

"Things change, Diana Rose," Rosemary said. "You haven't been home in a long time. Now you breeze in and breeze out. Shame on you for not even making the time to see your brothers. There's no good reason you can't stay one more day to see them and their families."

"There's no need to see them," Diana said in a cold voice. "Why in the world would they even care that I'm here?"

"Jim and Jarod are your family," Rosemary replied. "It would be good for their kids to see you once in their lifetime. You don't want to see the kids, fine. But your brothers are going to be helping me with Libby. For that reason alone, you should make time to see them."

The kitchen went quiet. Finally a chair scraped and Libby heard movement. She scrambled to her feet and went back to her room. She quickly put the suitcase on the floor and lay down on the bed. She listened hard to the murmur of voices. She couldn't understand what was said. The bedroom door opened and closed. She could smell her grandmother's powder and knew it wasn't her mother. Diana hadn't bothered to say goodbye. It was one more disappointment added to her pile of disappointments.

Rosemary watched her daughter's car disappear past the farmhouse where she'd been raised. Rosemary still puzzled about how she and James had raised such a child. Diana was a woman now but she was as selfish as ever. She was selfish enough to not risk saying goodbye to Libby because it would be too hard. She was selfish enough to walk away and expect her mother to handle the sad child she left behind.

Inside, she checked on her granddaughter. She was relieved to see that Libby was asleep. She closed the door softly and went to her own room. Lying down with her shoes on, she pulled a blanket over herself and stared at the ceiling until she heard Libby moving around. Then she got up, adjusted her clothing, and went across the hall to begin getting to know her granddaughter.

I was surprised when Libby asked me to be a witness for Christopher at his court hearing. I said sure, but the hearing came and without me knowing about it. I'd started teaching at the academy and lost touch with the goings-on at the station.

A call from Libby was the only way I knew what was happening with the kid.

"Detective Moran?" a woman's voice asked when I answered my cell phone. I didn't know the voice.

"Yes," I replied cautiously. I'd been teaching all day and was tired. I wasn't sure if I should know who this was and what she wanted.

"It's Libby," she said. "Elizabeth Lindt. From The Bertram House."

"Hi," I said. "Do you need me for court? I hope the hearing isn't this month. My schedule is pretty full for a while."

"It's over, she said. "He's on probation with hours and hours of community service. We've placed them in a great foster home."

"Probation," I said. "So somebody pressed charges, huh?"

"Yes," she replied. "One of the store owners thought it was the only way for him to understand consequences. In a way, I agree. His record will be sealed when he turns eighteen, so I think he'll be okay in the long run."

"That's great," I said. "And you placed them together. That's good."

"And it gets even better," Libby continued. "Their foster parents told me that they're ready to get out of the foster care rat race. They have four children placed with them, and they're going to adopt the kids they have now. After that, no more temporary foster placements for them."

"They're adopting four kids?" I asked.

"Yes," Libby said happily. "I'm so happy for him. No more living in cars. No more worrying where they'll end up next. And he and Molly are together. My two cents' worth is that it's the best thing that could happen to them."

"Congratulations," I said. "They must have been hard to place. You did good keeping them together."

"Well, it wasn't really me," she replied. "The judge's order said we had to find a place that would take both of them. I might have swayed him a tiny bit with my whining, but it was his order that did the trick."

"That's great," I said. "Thanks for letting me know what happened to them."

"Sure," she said. "I thought you'd like to know. And I wanted to thank you for your help. Do you come back here very often? I thought I'd treat you to ribs at Chucky's as a thank you. You know. Ribs. Cole slaw. A keg of beer.

"Well, maybe not a keg," I laughed. "You don't need to do that. I didn't do much."

"If I remember right," Libby said, "you apologized for something you didn't do. That apology helped Christopher more than you know. I'll trade you ribs for that thank you."

"Okay," I said. "I'll be back Friday afternoon. Should I pick you up?"

"Sure," she said. "But I want no argument about me paying for dinner. You can cover the tab next time."

Next time, I thought. There was going to be a next time.

Over ribs and beer, we decided we'd try every restaurant in town and do our own reviews of the food, complete with a one-to-five rating scale. We got a notebook to leave in my truck and for a few months we ate out a lot.

Not long after she treated me to ribs at Chucky's, Libby's building manager sent out a notice that he'd be recuperating from foot surgery for three weeks and wouldn't be available for repairs. He provided an alternate person for anything urgent but asked the tenants to wait for his return if they could. Libby's slow draining sink could technically wait for his return to duty, but it annoyed her enough that I offered to see what I could do.

It was my first visit to her apartment. Wearing jeans, polo shirt, and black running shoes, I carried my dad's toolbox through her living room to the kitchen. I noticed a flowered couch littered with pillows. A big green chair near the door looked like her favorite spot since books and magazines were stacked on the table next to it. I noticed movie posters on the walls, but I didn't take the time to really look at them.

The kitchen showed the age of the place with the once popular green appliances and matching sink. The room was so small I had to move the table into the living room so I could sit down and stretch out my legs.

"Do you need help in there?" Libby called from the bedroom where she'd gone to change clothes.

"I don't know yet," I called back. "But I do know I'm going to need a bucket. Do you have one handy?"

A minute later, I heard her front door open and footsteps go down the hall. I found the big red wrench in the toolbox and put my head under the sink. Libby appeared next to me with a two-gallon bucket and a handful of rags.

"Here goes nothing," I said.

I hate plumbing. I'm never sure I can put all the pieces back together. That means I'm never sure things won't leak with I'm done. And most of all, I hate the smell left behind in those hollow tubes we're so dependent on.

I loosened the fittings until I could maneuver the elbow joint away from the rest of the pipes. As I pulled it free, there was a small rush of water and a plunk in the bucket I'd positioned under the sink. Libby crouched next to me.

"What was that?" she asked.

"Sounded like a rock," I replied.

I tossed rags under the sink and pulled out the bucket. My forehead furrowed when I saw what was in the water.

"Yours?" I asked as I started to laugh.

"No," Libby said as she looked in the bucket and laughed with me. "Not mine."

It wasn't that funny, but before long, we were holding our sides. A spoon with the Disney logo and a worn Mickey Mouse head had gotten caught at the pipe joint and was blocking the water. I got up from the floor and together we peered down the drain.

"How do you think that happened?" I asked.

Libby gingerly wiped the spoon dry and fitted it into the strainer. Neither the logo handle nor the Mickey bowl fit through the slots. How the spoon got in the pipes was a mystery.

"Gremlins?" Libby asked. "Disney magic?"

"Gremlins," I nodded seriously. "There's no other answer."

I slid back under the sink and put the pipes together. We ran water to check for leaks before I reloaded Dad's toolbox and set it by the front door. Then we moved the table and chairs back into the kitchen.

Libby opened the refrigerator and handed me a beer and a plastic mixing bowl. She pointed to the living room as she reached back and brought out the same for herself. She followed me to the couch. I settled at one end with my legs across the cushions. She sat at the other end, stretched her feet toward me, and rested her legs between mine.

"What's this?" I asked, looking in the bowl.

"My version of a chef salad," Libby replied. "I believe in protein. You'll find two kinds of lettuce, two kinds of cheese, turkey, ham, boiled eggs and a few cranberries along with tomato wedges. It's my favorite Saturday supper."

"Who showed you your way around the kitchen?" I asked. "Your mother?"

"No, not my mother," she replied. "I learned some from my grandmother, but mostly I just sort of picked things up when I needed to."

"But you do have a mother, right," I asked.

I surprised myself by pushing this. I'd told her about my family, even how I was inspired by Uncle Glenn and about how I was afraid of Marta when she was a teenager. But Libby hadn't said much about hers.

"Yes, I do have a mother, Tanner," Libby replied, making a funny face at me. "I just don't talk about her like you talk about your family."

"I'm going to have to know eventually," I said, raising an eyebrow. "You might as well tell me now. And I don't care who your family is or what they've done. I want to know more about you, that's all."

Libby nodded but didn't say anything. I waited. I figured she was organizing her thoughts. I loaded my fork with ham, cheese, and lettuce while I waited. The bite was crisp. The dressing had a light sweet-and-sour after-bite. It was a great meal.

"Short and not so sweet," she said, poking my leg with her toe. "I have...had one sister. Megan. She was two years younger than me. My father took her in a divorce/custody thing when I was eleven. I haven't seen either of them since. I lived with my grandmother for two years after that. My mother would probably have left me with Gram forever but she had to go into assisted living because of her hip."

"She would have left you there?" I asked. "What does that mean?"

"My Mom was never much of a mother," Libby sighed. "She thinks about herself than she thinks about anyone or anything else. And she has a mean streak I'm glad I'm not around anymore. But my two cents' worth is that she did the best she could. She is alive and well and living in Boston."

We ate in silence before she continued.

"I have two very good friends, Susan and Connie, who have been with me since grade school. One of my mother's boyfriends christened us the Three Musketeers when we were in junior high, and we're still close enough to claim the title. Those two are really my family. You'll meet them eventually."

My cop radar hummed. I didn't want our talk to turn into an interrogation, but I wanted to keep her talking. I loaded my fork again.

"So your mother remarried when you were a kid?" I asked before I took my next bite.

"Oh, yes, eventually" Libby said. "I'd have to have paper and pencil to figure it out, but I think she might be on number eleven or twelve. She didn't marry all of them, but we lived with quite of few of them. Alan Ross is her current husband. My two cents' worth is that Al's a great guy. I'm betting she'll finish with him by the end of the year and be out looking for the next guy on New Year's Eve. I don't know how she does it, but she always finds a new man when she wants one."

"And you don't know where your father is?" I asked.

"Nope," she replied. She started talking very fast, keeping her sentences short. "My parents were at the end of a very bitter divorce. We were in the kitchen fixing dinner the day Meg disappeared. I was making macaroni and cheese from a box. Can you believe that? Macaroni from a box. Megan was cutting tomatoes. Dad wasn't supposed to get near us by then. Mom said to never open the door for him. But he just waltzed through the kitchen door without knocking. He called us Babies just like he always did. And he took my sister with him when he left. I think he tried to use Meg as leverage in the divorce but it didn't work."

Libby looked at the ceiling a took a deep breath. I took a swallow of my beer.

"And you never saw your sister again," I said.

"Nope," Libby said again. Her voice was back to normal and I let her talk without interruption. "At first, I was sure he'd bring her back. I thought they'd work things out and Meg would come back when Dad didn't need her anymore. I don't know what my mother did, but whatever it was he was so angry that he kept Meg. My two cents' worth is that they both died before Meg was old enough to come back on her own. I can't figure out anything else that makes sense. She would have come back if she could."

She paused and we ate in silence for a while. Then she continued thoughtfully.

"Connie, Susan, and I used to spend hours talking about it and trying to figure out a way for me to get in touch with Dad. For a long time I thought if I could just find them I could convince him to let Meg come back to Mom and me. But that was wishful thinking. And we spent hours on the computer. They disappeared long before there was a web, but once we knew about it....well, let's just say the three of us left no stone unturned. At one point, I even hired a PI to look for them."

"What about your mother?" I asked. "What did she do?"

"Only two things that I know of," Libby replied. "She filed a police report when it first happened and she ran an ad in the newspapers for a while after the divorce was final asking him to bring her baby back. Nothing happened either time. As Meg's father, he had every right to keep her. And my mother wasn't the best one I've known, so I think the police didn't do much to find them. My two cents' worth is that after dealing with my mother for so long Dad might have decided he was doing what was best for Meg."

"And he didn't think about his kids and how you two were affected by it," I said softly.

"Whatever he thought he was doing, it didn't work," Libby said sadly. "We had to move out of the house because Mom couldn't afford it after he left. She sold our furniture and the car. When we cleaned out the house, she tossed everything Dad left behind. I didn't know it at the time, but she put Meg's things in a box. I found it at my grandmother's after she went into assisted living."

Libby almost smiled. I guessed she still had that box someplace. We ate in silence for a while. I finished my salad and set the bowl on the floor. I took her feet in my hands and found them cold under the socks.

"I know three things," she said. "One, my parents were the worst parents ever. Two, my father grabbed the kid who was closest to the kitchen door. And three, I will never see Megan again. The first two are over and I'm not too mad about them anymore. But every now and then the last one wakes me up at night and I'm mad all over again. My two cents' worth is that I will be a little bit angry with them for the rest of my life."

We sat quiet on the couch with our legs entwined as we finished our beers. I rubbed her feet while she thought about her parents. I knew I would eventually offer to do what I could to find Megan, but it wasn't the time for that. For now, I just enjoyed the feel of this wonderful lady and a full stomach.

When she heard the squeal of brakes, Rosemary looked up from the cake she was decorating. Libby bounded down the bus steps followed by Sara and Jeff from the farm house next door. They walked together to Rosemary's cottage, the three of them talking a mile a minute. Then Sara and Jeff veered off and ran to the farmhouse.

"Guess what?" Libby called as the door slammed behind her.

"You learned to close a door today," Rosemary called back.

"No," Libby said. She stopped at the kitchen doorway and looked at Rosemary's project. "Wow, Gram. That's beautiful."

"It is, isn't it?" Rosemary stepped back for a better view of her creation.

The four-layer wedding cake was a lace castle with white roses lining the top of each layer and a miniature sugar trellis on top waiting for the plastic bride and groom.

"What kind?' Libby asked. "Will you teach me how?"

"It's just plain white cake," Rosemary replied. She walked around the table with a critical eye on the cake. "I can teach you when you're ready. But you're too busy now to start learning this. It takes a lot of practice."

"Oh, that's what I was going to tell you," Libby said. "We have to get some running shoes. I joined the cross-country track team today."

"Cross country?" Rosemary asked. She smiled at Libby's flushed face. "What's that?"

"I don't know," Libby laughed. "Sara and me like to run. Her Dad said we can run around the pasture and the corn field as long as we stay close to the fence. He said absolutely no running down the corn rows. So we joined the team today."

"Hmm," Rosemary said. "And you need special shoes to run."

"Yes," Libby said. "I need them by Monday. Sara said her mother can take us on Saturday. You won't need to go unless you want to."

"Hmm," Rosemary said again.

Diana had not come back for her daughter at summer's end. Instead, two days before she was to be there, Rosemary got a hysterical call. Diana couldn't stop crying long enough to explain what was happening. Rosemary sent her oldest son to Kingsford Grove. Jarod moved his sister to a rehab facility. He packed up her apartment and brought her boxes back with him

Two months later, rehab completed and the tears dried, Diana called again to ask Rosemary to keep Libby for the school year. She wasn't ready to handle the stress of raising her daughter. Rosemary thought Diana was simply being her selfish self. She also thought that for the time being Libby was better off where she was. So Jarod went back with Diana's boxes and helped her find a new apartment. Now Rosemary didn't know when Libby would be going back to her mother and her old life.

"Gram?" Libby asked, waving her hand in front of Rosemary's face.

"Hmm," Rosemary replied. She blinked her eyes and focused on Libby.

"Where'd you go?" Libby laughed. "When do they pick up the cake? Where are we going to eat tonight?"

Rosemary pulled the girl into a hug.

"The bakery truck is supposed to be here before 5:30 pm," she said as she smoothed Libby's curly hair. "But you two can eat in front of the television if you want even if the cake's gone by then. You're having burgers and fries. And you can use the mixer to make shakes if you want. When is Sara coming?"

"In a while," Libby replied. "She has to help with the chickens, but then she'll be here. She's bringing a sleeping bag."

Rosemary smiled as she watched Libby run the short distance to her room.

Tanner parked his car behind Libby's. He made sure the building's entry door clicked shut behind him and then climbed the stairs to the familiar door on the second floor. Libby opened it at his knock.

"You look tired," she said. "Sit. I'll get you a beer."

Tanner sank back in the soft couch pillows and sighed. He thought this couch might be the most comfortable piece of furniture he'd ever sat in. He wasn't crazy about the big pink flowers, but it was comfortable.

"This is great," he smiled as Libby handed him a sweating bottle. "You've made quite a home here."

"Get comfortable." Libby smiled back. "I'm going to change clothes and put dinner on the table. Turn on the television if you want to."

He took a swallow of beer and set the bottle on the floor. He leaned forward, untied his shoes, and slid his feet out of them. As he took off his jacket, he wiggled his toes, and sighed again. He put the jacket on the cushion next to him, picked up his beer, and settled back into the pillows. He listened to Libby's activity as he sipped beer. He liked the sounds of someone taking care of him. He stretched out his legs and looked at a hole in the toe of the sock on his left foot.

A while later Libby walked back to the living room. She smiled at Tanner's sleeping frame, head back on a cushion, feet akimbo in front of him, beer bottle tucked safely under the table. She knelt in front of him and gently shook his knees. His eyes opened slowly. He looked around in confusion until his eyes settled on her. He smiled. She stood up and held out a hand.

"Dinner's ready, Mr. Moran," she said.

He took the offered hand and she made a production of pulling him to his feet. As he put his arm around her shoulders, a large cat paused in the bedroom doorway to watch them. Tanner raised an eyebrow at Libby.

"Yours?" he asked.

"Tanner, meet Big Boy," Libby said with a smile. "He comes and goes on his own schedule, so I never know when he's going to be here."

She leaned down to stroke the cat before going to the kitchen.

Plates of mini meatloaves with Caesar salads were on the table. A glass of wine sat with one plate, a beer with the other. Tanner sat down and forked a bite of meatloaf into his mouth. Libby grinned at him while she opened a can of tuna, dumped it into a bowl, and set it on the floor. Tanner shook his head as she sat down from him.

"Still can't believe I can cook a real meal?" she asked.

"I can't believe you have a cat," he replied. "All this time, and you never told me you have a cat."

"My two cents' worth is that he has me," Libby said. "One night I was curled up in bed reading when I heard thudding on my siding door. Big Boy was on the deck knocking to get in. Since then he shows up every now and then, stays for a day or a week, and then wanders off until the next time."

"He knocked on the door to your deck?" Tanner asked. "You're on the second floor."

"I know," Libby replied with a grin. "I have no idea why he picked me. And I have no idea how he gets up there, but he does. And he butts his head against the door until I let him in. I've started keeping grilled chicken in the freezer and cans of tuna in the cupboard so I have something to feed him."

"Hmm," Tanner said. The meatloaf was spicy and the salad perfectly crisp. Under the table, Libby rested her bare feet on top of Tanner's stockinged ones. The cat lay Sphinx-like in the doorway watching the action.

When their plates were empty, Tanner took them to the sink while Libby put out slices of cheesecake and cups of coffee. Big Boy jumped onto Tanner's lap as soon as he returned to his chair. He pushed his cheesecake away before using both hands to rub the cat.

"He's big," Tanner said. "What do you think? Twenty-five, thirty pounds?"

"At least thirty," Libby replied. "I've never seen a cat that big except on The Nature Channel. And look at his ears. They look like bobcat ears, don't they? I think he likes you."

Tanner gently scooted the cat off his lap and went to the sink to wash his hands.

"Just so you know," he said as he sat back down and reached for his dessert. "I'm not really a pet person."

"That's okay," Libby replied over her coffee cup. "This cat is not really a pet. I feed him when he shows up, but I don't do litter boxes and he doesn't need one."

"Uh, huh," Tanner said. "How are you going to let him know where you are when you move in with me?"

"We're moving in together?" Libby asked. She tilted her head and batted her eyelashes.

"I thought we might," Tanner said with a grin. "We get along. We make each other laugh. We don't fight much. I think it's time we make it permanent."

Libby put her fork down, crossed her arms on the table, and leaned forward.

"So you're asking me to marry you?" she asked, keeping her expression blank.

"Well," Tanner stammered. "We can decide that later. We can get married if you still want to after you know me better."

Libby continued to lean forward with a straight face. She widened her eyes and kept her eyes on his.

"I'll pay for a big, fancy wedding if you decide you want one," he said, stammering again. "I mean, if that's what you want when you know me better, I can do that."

She nodded and watched a deep flush rise from his collar. She rested her chin on one hand and batted her eyelashes again.

"How big of a wedding?" she asked, struggling not to laugh at Tanner's expression.

"However big you want," he said. "All I need is to be with you. Married or not, I want to start and end my days with you in my arms."

Libby leaned back and picked up her cup. Tanner watched her. Under the table the cat circled their legs. Libby smiled and shook her head.

"This place is too small for the two of us on a permanent basis," she said. "And your place is even smaller. Do you think you'd be willing to maybe rent a house instead of paying for a big wedding?"

Tanner pushed his plate away. His face returned to normal as he leaned back in his chair. Big boy jumped onto his lap and curled into a ball. Tanner let out a breath and ran his fingers through the soft fur.

"Okay," he said. He smiled at her. "If you want a house, we can look at houses. But if we aren't going to live in an apartment, I want to break with family tradition."

What family tradition is that?" Libby asked.

"My parents rented until Randall and I left home," Tanner explained "Randy and Marta both rent their houses. But I want to buy something. If we've going to have a new life then we can have our own traditions."

Libby got up and stood in front of him. He rested his hands on her hips as she leaned in to give him a gentle kiss. Stray, curly hair brushed his skin.

"Okay," she said, her breath soft against his lips. "We'll have our own traditions."

Part 2

*L*ibby pulled a second chair close to hers. Around her, volunteers and advocates opened take-out bags and set cups on the conference table. She stretched her legs across the chair, briefly touched her toes to flex her tight back muscles, and unwrapped her sandwich.

"Let's get started," Sam Hayes, Director of The Bertram House, said. "Late comers will have to get their information from you all."

There was a flurry of activity as papers rustled, chairs were pulled out then scooted in, and everyone settled down. Libby took a bite of her sandwich. She set it on the plastic wrap and picked up her pen. She regularly took notes for her friends since she was at every meeting. This time Connie was on deadline at work and wouldn't make the meeting. Susan had called to let Libby know she'd be late.

"We've got two empty rooms," Sam started. "That's five beds. I personally hope they're not needed for a while." He pointed his pen at a lanky man sitting next to Libby. "Howard, can you get those rooms painted this week?"

Howard Michaels, a retired contractor who volunteered at BB's and several shelters in the city, had kept Bertram's ancient house in repair for all the years Libby had worked there. It was his old network that got most of the materials he needed donated to BB's and the other charities.

"If someone can move the furniture I'll be back to tape on Thursday afternoon. I can paint Friday and Saturday. Let the rooms dry on Sunday and you can move the furniture back where it belongs on Monday."

Sam nodded and made a note on the TO DO list that sat in front of him. After the meeting, the list would be posted on a bulletin board outside his office and the people doing the work would either check their task off as completed or leave Sam a note if there was a problem. It was a simple system, but it worked well with the volunteers' odd schedules.

"Libby, can you update us on the Founder's Day plans?" Sam asked.

"Sure," Libby replied. "The room's reserved at the Holiday Inn, graciously paid for by Mrs. Cochran again this year. Food donations are coming in. We're storing things in the kitchen for now and the perishables will be delivered to the Holiday Inn the morning of the event. We need two more fire fighters to volunteer to cook, but if no one does, Susan and Connie's husbands have agreed to step in. I believe the only loose end is making sure all of our wait staff have white shirts and black pants."

"I'm handling that," a woman at the end of the table put in. "Sears donated gift certificates and I'm taking the last three kids to the mall after school on Friday. Just so you know, I've allowed each kid to get one thing they want as a reward for helping out at the dinner."

"Like what?" Sam asked as he made notes on his list.

"Melissa got silver hoop earrings. Robert wanted neon orange laces for his high tops," she smiled at the group. "Things like that. And I'll be using another of the mall vouchers to feed them while we're there."

"How many vouchers do we have left?" Sam asked.

"Five or six," she replied. "I'll solicit more when we get down to three. The mall has been great about it."

"How's the fundraising coming?" Sam looked at a blonde at the far end of the table.

The woman smiled at Libby before starting her story about Connie and Susan's presentation at the Elks' Club Breakfast and their update of The Bertram House web site.

"The money isn't pouring in," she said. "But the Elk's gave us $5,000 and individual members are making donations. We've had requests for perpetuity information. I think we'll be included in a couple of wills, so there will be money down the line. We're on the agenda for the Eagles and Kiwanis next month. They both gave us large donations last year."

Susan arrived and took the chair next to Libby who tipped her notes so Susan could see what had happened so far. The meeting went on for the lunch hour and a little longer. Their discussion included budget, marketing, current court cases, and the advocate application that was being modified. Sam asked for any concerns that hadn't been discussed. Then he adjourned the meeting.

"Did you talk with Tanner about coming to dinner on Sunday?" Susan asked as she unlocked the car and slid behind the wheel.

"I did," Libby replied. "We'll be there at noon. But my two cents' worth is that you need to spread the word for everyone to be on their best behavior. I don't want you to scare him on your first encounter. There will be plenty of time for all of you to interrogate him later. What can I bring?"

Susan laughed and put her right hand over her heart.

"I promise we'll behave," she said. "You are in charge of bread this time. Bring something good."

She closed the car door and waved as she drove away."

"But why?" Libby said into the phone. "Why can't I come home?"

It was a slow August afternoon. Rosemary sat in front of a fan knitting a striped cap for the church rummage sale. Libby had been reading beside her since it was too hot to be outside.

"I miss my friends," Rosemary heard a sob in Libby's voice. "How can we stay friends if I don't see them?"

Libby was quiet as she listened to Diana. Rosemary was sure her daughter was surprised when Libby answered. If Diana had known Libby was allowed to answer the phone, she wouldn't have called until she thought her daughter was in bed.

"But you're my mother," Libby wailed. "I should live with you. You should act like my mother."

There was another long silence as Libby listened. Then Rosemary heard the receiver settle in its cradle and the back door slam. She stood up and hobbled to the kitchen. From the window she could see Libby running on the tractor path inside the cornfield fence.

Rosemary went back to her knitting and waited. She remembered her own kids at thirteen. Thirteen seemed to be the magic age when kids started separating, started challenging their parents. And Libby was two months shy of thirteen. So far nothing had happened between the two of them, but Rosemary knew it was coming. It had to happen in order for Libby to grow up.

She was just starting to worry when her granddaughter came through the kitchen and stood in front of her. There were dusty tear streams down her flushed cheeks and her curly hair was wild around her head. The knees of her jeans had dry mud patches on them as though she'd fallen. Rosemary put her knitting down and patted the cushion next to her.

"She hates me." Libby began sobbing as she plunked herself down on the couch. "Why does she hate me?"

Rosemary pulled her granddaughter close and held her while she cried. She kissed the girl's warm cheek and stroked her hair until she stopped crying.

"She doesn't hate you," Rosemary said softly. "I know it feels like that, but she really doesn't hate you."

"Then why doesn't she want me?" Libby asked.

"Have you noticed that she doesn't usually call unless I call her first? I call and leave a message for her to call back?" Rosemary asked. "And when she does call, you're in bed?

"Yeah. So?" Libby said.

"How long have you been here?"

"Almost two years," Libby replied.

"And how many times has she been to see you?"

"None," Libby said in a small voice.

Rosemary pushed Libby away from her and turned the girl so they were eye-to-eye.

"None," Rosemary repeated. "She has not made that short three-hour drive in two years. Any decent mother would have come to see you a dozen times by now." She took hold of Libby's ears and kissed one cheek and then the other. "Any decent mother would call to talk to her daughter every week. This is not your fault, Honey. Do you hear me? This is not your fault."

Rosemary moved Libby until she was sitting between her knees. She started playing with Libby's hair while she talked.

"You mother was always selfish," Rosemary continued thoughtfully. "Almost as soon as she could talk, she was demanding things. All kids do that, but she was different. She was so different from your uncles when she was growing up. She didn't keep friends unless she could boss them around or they could do something for her. She didn't help anyone unless she absolutely had to. Oh, she helped if it made her look good but never just to do something for someone. And she was mean to the people around her."

She had braided Libby's hair. She used her fingers to comb it out again. Then she twisted it into a tight spiral on the back of her head. Her fingers combed it out again.

"It used to hurt me that she didn't love me," Rosemary said. "Even when she was little, she didn't have any use for her father or me or her brothers. That hurt a lot. But I finally figured out there wasn't anything she could do about it. She was born that way. She didn't ask to be like that. And she didn't work to be so self-centered. It just happened."

Absently, she twisted Libby's hair into a spiral again and held it against the back of Libby's head. She picked up a knitting needle and carefully pushed it through the twist. She patted it and turned her granddaughter around to face her.

"You are not selfish," Rosemary said. She held Libby's face in her hands and looked her in the eye. "And you're not mean. You have a big heart and a big laugh and lots of people love you. If your mom doesn't, it's too bad for her. She's missing something good not spending time with you."

"But she's the mom," Libby said softly. She sniffled and rested her forehead on Rosemary's.

"I know," Rosemary said. "But she doesn't understand what that means. Unfortunately, you have to be the one who understands. You get to be the one who makes the effort. She just can't do any better, Honey. And she'll always do mean things that will hurt your feelings if you let them. She can't understand. But you're strong enough to figure out what needs to be done and do it."

Libby looked at her grandmother and sighed. She was comforted by her grandmother's warmth and the baby powder smell of her clothes. But what she said didn't change anything.

"Am I ever going home?" she asked. "Connie and Susan won't stay my friends forever if they can't see me. We're The Three Musketeers. We won't be if I don't get to go home before they forget me."

"You will go home," Rosemary said. "I don't know when, but you will. And we can have your friends here again for a visit this summer. You can be The Four Musketeers with Sara."

"Okay," Libby said. She touched her hair. "What did you do?"
"Go and look," Rosemary smiled. "I like it."

For a while, we spent our Saturdays looking at houses. I leaned toward simple ramblers in housing developments. I liked that everything was new and wouldn't break for a few years. The yard would be new, so the plants wouldn't need pruning. I'd have to mow the lawn and that was about it. New developments might seem sterile to some people, but for me they are the best and easiest way to go. And, if you buy a house before it's built, you get to pick your floor plan and colors. I liked that, too.

Libby went along with this for a few weekends, but before long I realized she was looking for something quite different from the houses I liked. After looking at a dozen or so new homes, she told me we could do better. When she showed up at my apartment mid-morning the next Saturday, she brought the classifieds ads with three red circles and a bag filled with food. I looked at the addresses in the ads and thought the day would be a loss.

The houses in the ads were barely within the city limits in a worn-down part of town known for midnight visits by the black-and-whites. I couldn't imagine any of them were worth looking at. The houses I'd seen out there were old. I knew some of them dated back to WWII. As far as I was concerned, they would be more work than they were worth.

But Libby had been willing to look at my idea of where we should live, so I figured the least I could do was see what she had in mind. If nothing else, we might come to a meeting of the minds on what to look at next.

The first house on her list was probably not even nine hundred square feet, including the lean-to that served as a garage. Its paint was peeling and the lawn was worn down to dirt. We walked around the place and peeked in windows both front and back. Inside we saw cracked linoleum and shag carpet that had seen better days. Without a single comment, we got in the truck and I drove to the next address.

It was another rambler, newer by a few years, and the outside showed much better upkeep. Still, when we hooded our eyes and looked inside, I cringed at the mess we'd be spending good money to clean up. Wallpaper hung in strips from walls browned with old glue, the floors were bare except for the nail boards along the walls, and three of the rooms were missing light fixtures. The size was better, though, and I might have considered it if the inside wasn't such a mess.

"One more," Libby said. She took my hand and we walked back to the truck.

I got behind the wheel, but for a minute Libby stood with her back to the truck and looked around the yard again. A thick braid was piled high on her head and secured with pins I couldn't see. She wore faded jeans, a red sweatshirt, and bright white tennis shoes. I was thinking about the feel of my hands on her hips when she turned and got in the truck.

"Listen," she said as she clicked the seatbelt across her lap. "I know you want something newer. But my two cents' worth is that I'd like more of a yard than what we've been looking at. I like to garden. I'm thinking that one of these older houses will be in good enough shape that we won't have to do too much work to get it in shape. And it will have a yard I can revitalize."

"Libby, we both work long hours," I said. "I think we should get something that won't take a lot of our time."

"I would agree with that," she began. "Except that I have to have something to do when I'm home alone. You're going to be sleeping in a dorm with other guys half the time. I need to be busy when you're gone. If not, I'll spend all my time thinking about work. I like getting my hands dirty. And when I do, my mind wanders away and my body relaxes. I solve all kinds of problems when I'm working in the dirt."

"Maybe so," I said. "But these houses have such big yards that I don't think the two of us working together for a year could get one straightened up. Besides, I'm not much for yard work."

She'd lived in an apartment the whole time I'd known her, so I didn't understand yet that she used yard work as therapy, used it as her way to forget for a little while the harshness of the system she worked in.

"You don't need to be," she smiled at me. I melted a little at that smile. "If you absolutely need to help, we can have grass for you to mow. Everything else will be up to me."

I gave her a skeptical look and she gave me the next address.

"One more, okay?" she asked. "Then we can find someplace to eat."

The last house of the day was a bright, oversized Craftsman sitting on a corner lot across from another Craftsman on a corner lot. It was attractively painted with three different colors on its ornate trim. As I pulled into the gravel driveway cutting a circular corner off the lot, I cringed at the idea of painting all the little curlicues on the trim. True, it looked great now. The house was shiny with new paint and the work would be postponed for a few years. But I didn't like the idea of the job anywhere in my future. I gave Libby a skeptical look and opened my door.

Libby got out slowly, shading her face to look at the house. It sat level with the driveway, but I could see a slight slope along one side that lead to the back of the house. I walked across the small lawn and up the stairs to look in the windows. Libby headed to the corner of the house and the backyard.

The new front door was unstained wood. Three narrow rectangular windows ended a third of the way down the door and a brass doorknocker was fixed below each one. The largest doorknocker, a front facing dragon's head, was under the middle window. Beneath the others, dragons of different designs forked their tongues out to greet visitors. I tried each of them in turn and heard the knocking echo through the house. The sound made me smile.

I framed my face against a window and looked inside. No damage. No missing carpet. No bare wires hanging from the ceiling. A staircase ended close to the front door. I could see through the living room into the kitchen. Both rooms looked clean and as newly painted as the outside. Most intriguing from where I stood was a fireplace at the end of one wall with light coming through the hearth. It had been a long time since I'd seen a two-faced fireplace, but it looked like this house had one.

I turned around and went to find Libby. She had walked down the slope beside the house and across the backyard to a tilted, waist-high picket fence that had seen better years. Beyond the fence I could see rows of trees in a jumble of undergrowth.

"Apple trees," she said as I joined her. I wrapped my arms around her shoulders and pulled her close. I nodded into her hair even though I couldn't tell an apple from an elm.

"This is all you'll need to mow," she said, indicating the area between the house and the fence. "This and the little bit of grass in the front of the house. It's not too much, do you think?"

"No," I said as I let go of her. "It's not too much for me to mow. But this is a big house, Libby. We don't need anything this big. And look at the yard. I bet there are at least two acres here. Are you sure we need something like this?"

"We don't even need a house," she laughed. She put an arm around my waist and gave me a squeeze. "I do believe we would be all right anywhere we're together."

I gave her my skeptical look again. She reached up and patted my cheek.

"Did you look inside?" she asked.

"I did," I replied. "There are three door knockers on the front door."

"Three?" she asked.

"Three," I said. "Dragons. They're nice dragons, too. And there's a fireplace. It looks like it warms two rooms."

"I've never heard of that," Libby said.

"I've seen a few," I replied. "They're double faced with hearths on two sides of the wall. The other side of this one is probably in a bedroom."

We walked to the back of the house and looked in the window on the bottom floor. The slope created a daylight basement under the two stories visible from the street. Inside was a large room that could be used for just about anything. We could see a large galvanized sink against one wall and a shower stall in the corner under the stairs on the far side of the room.

Libby linked her arm in mine, and we walked back up the slope and around the house to the front steps. She rubbed the largest doorknocker and then tried it out just as I had. We peeked through the windows into the main room on the first floor.

Neither of us said anything as I drove through town to the campground at the river. I parked under a willow tree and carried our lunch to a picnic table. Libby got out of the truck, walked down to the river, and skipped rocks across the slow moving water. I sat leaning back with my elbows on the table and watched her. No matter how much I practiced, I could never get a rock to skip more than twice. She had them going four and five hops before they sank.

We were giving each other time to think about the house. I knew she wanted it. I'd seen it in her eyes when she told me about the apple trees. I also knew where we lived didn't make much difference to me. She was right to say I'd be spending most of my time at the academy. I knew I'd be sleeping in the dorm for a few nights every week when training was in session and driving back and forth even if I wasn't teaching. At most, I'd be home two or three nights each week for the next three or four years.

She walked slowly to the table and started taking food out of the bag. She unwrapped a sandwich of thick roast beef and tomato slices and put it in front of me. Then she opened Tupperware containers of crinkle chips and sliced carrots and celery, put them in the middle of the table, and set out napkins. She opened a small thermos of what smelled like my barley soup for herself. We ate in silence for a bit before we started talking about the house.

"I liked it," she finally said.

I nodded and chewed. Strands of her thick hair had come loose from the braid and a breeze blew them around her head. The bright sun had her squinting so I couldn't see her eyes clearly.

"It was one of the best ones so far," I agreed. "But I have two concerns. One, it's too far out. When you get called in the middle of the night, you're going to be on a two-lane road to get back to your office or the police station. In the middle of the night, that may not be safe. And two, it's way too big for us. It's just you and me, Babe. We don't need half that space. And two acres of yard? That's a lot to take care of."

Libby spooned soup into her mouth and crunched a chip. She looked at the river.

"We need to see the inside," she said. "If there's a room on the main floor we can use as a bedroom, we won't need to do anything with the upstairs. We can live on the main floor and I can use the basement for my garden shed."

"I didn't know you liked gardening," I commented. "I know you said you did last week, but that's the first I've heard of it."

"Well, I do. You don't know because we both live in apartments," she said. "But if I didn't have to work for a living, I'd be out in the dirt every day."

"You could do that in any of the other houses we looked at," I said. "New developments have dirt, too, you know."

"Those houses are so close together," she replied. "I like the idea of being in a place with neighbors close enough to call if you need them but far enough away that you have privacy. That's how this one felt to me."

"Maybe, I said. "But it's too far out. I'm not home every night. You're going to be alone at least three nights every week, sometimes four. I'd be more comfortable if you were closer in."

"Closer to what?" she asked. "We'd still be in the city limits. Wherever we are, if something happens, I'll call 911 and wait. My two cents' worth is that the response time can't be that different between any of the developments and that house."

"The maintenance is going to be a killer," I said. "Did you see all those curlicues on the roofline? There is no way I can paint those at my age. Can you imagine me up on a ladder?"

Libby laughed. We ate and looked at the water for a while. She put her thermos away, closed the Tupperware, and threw my sandwich wrap in the bag. Then she handed me a fork and another Tupperware container. I opened it to find a rather large piece of her double chocolate cake with oversized frosting roses piped into the corners of the container. The first bite of any of Libby's confections is heaven. The rest of the bites aren't too bad, either.

We didn't talk as we spread a blanket in the sun and stretched out. We watched the wind blow clouds across the sky, now and then pointing out shapes we saw in them. Libby fell asleep with her head on my shoulder. By the time she woke up and we headed home, I knew I'd be buying the house with a million curlicues that would need to be painted in a few years.

Libby didn't ask me to see what I could find out about Meg's disappearance. I guessed this was because her friends' efforts and those of the investigator she'd hired had convinced her nothing was going to change. She'd accepted that her Dad and sister were gone. She seemed to have settled it with herself.

It bothered me, though, so I finally asked Uncle Glenn if he remembered a case like that from his years with the police department. He didn't, but he said he'd talk with his friends and see if he could learn anything. Maybe since the case was so old, he might be able to borrow the file if he asked the right people. He said to give him a week. We made a date for dinner at his house and I went off to the academy.

The next weekend, my first stop in town was KFC for Uncle Glenn's favorite chicken dinner. Then I went to see what he'd found out.

The apartment above my parent's garage is nicer than mine. Mom redecorated it before Uncle Glenn moved in, and it has lots of light from windows on two sides. I always smiled when I saw the huge green asparagus fern he's so proud of. He'd rigged a spotlight in the corner of the dining space to focus on the plant. He'd modified a tomato cage and stuck it in the pot so the fern's fronds were lifted about six inches above the dirt. From there they grew nearly to the floor and filled the corner.

He didn't hear my knock or the door open since he was vacuuming. He jumped when I deliberately slammed the door to let him I was there. He held up a finger and finished what he was doing. I got down plates, found silverware, and set out the food. After he put the vacuum away and washed his hands, he joined me at the table.

"I don't think you're going to like this," he said without preamble.

He pushed an old file folder across the table to me. He put potatoes and gravy on his plate, than added a chicken thigh while he talked.

"Once I started asking questions, I remembered this case," he said. "I didn't work it but all of us knew about the woman back then. She was one a cold fish. That's what I remembered when I heard the guys talk about the case. Her only concern was that the accident didn't show up in the papers."

"What do you mean?' I asked.

"She didn't seem to care that two people she supposedly loved were dead," Uncle Glenn replied. "She just didn't want the deaths announced in the papers. She asked about that over and over."

"Why would she care about that?" I asked, thinking out loud. "I can't see that it would make any difference."

"She said it would disrupt her life if the neighbors knew what happened," he replied.

"So I need to read what's in here?" I asked, shaking my head.

"Yeah," he said. "I think you should. But I'll give you the Cliff Notes version. The parents were getting a divorce. The husband moves out. The wife gets the house but she has trouble holding things together. The usual stuff. Not enough money. The mortgage is more than she could afford."

I nodded. Libby told me that much.

"For some reason, the wife gets a restraining order on the husband," Uncle Glenn continued. "But he shows up when she isn't home. From what the older girl, Libby I guess, told us back then, her father must have waited outside someplace watching the house. Soon as the wife leaves, he goes in the back door. Anyways, he takes one of the girls with him when he leaves. Does any of this sound familiar?"

"All of it," I said. "So far, it's pretty much what Libby knows."

"They got their divorce," he continued between bites of chicken. "The wife says she begged him to bring the girl back, but he didn't. Instead it looks like he was taking her up to Smithfield where he had a new job and a new apartment the wife didn't know about."

"How do you know that?" I asked. "Libby doesn't know anything after he took Meg from the kitchen."

"She might not know, but her mother does," Uncle Glenn said. "The report says she was told all this after the accident."

"What accident?" I ask.

"Car accident," he replied. "The man must have been doing over eighty on the river road, headed north. Lost control on that second bridge outside Purdue Junction."

"Damn," I said. "They drowned."

"Trapped in the car," Uncle Glenn nodded. "It looked like they were in the water a couple of days before anyone saw the car."

"And you're sure it was them?" I asked

"The car tags were right," he said. "The ID in his wallet matched the registration. Besides, the wife identified them."

"Libby's mother identified them?" I asked. I leaned forward in my chair, my eyes wide at this news. "When?"

"Right after the car was found," he replied. "As soon as the morgue had them ready, the detectives brought her in for a talk before asking her to identify them. She took the bag of girls' clothes. Sshe didn't want anything of his, so I guess everything else went to the incinerator."

I pushed my plate away and opened the file. Uncle Glenn ate while I scanned the papers. There was a picture of the car with bodies and floating groceries inside. Another of two bodies under tarps on the riverbank. There were picture of bags containing clothes in the trunk. And Diana Lindt's signature was on the form releasing her husband and daughter's bodies to the funeral home. I shook my head in disgust and closed the file.

"You're sure Libby doesn't know about this?" Uncle Glenn asked.

"She doesn't know," I said, rubbing a hand over my jaw. "Her mother never told her."

"Well, the woman has obviously known for a long time," he said. "Have you met her?"

"Libby's mother? No," I replied. "Libby said I'd meet her and her new husband at the wedding. We did have dinner with her uncles, Jim and Jarod. They're both nice guys. One's a pharmacist. The other one does land development for contractors. I liked them."

"I bet she never told them either," Uncle Glenn said, shaking his head. "I bet she kept it secret from everyone. Who would do that? Maybe she thought if nobody knew they'd feel sorry for her."

"It gets worse," I said. "Libby says that her mother keeps asking if she's talked with Megan. She knows the girl's dead and for twenty years every time they talk, she asks Libby if she's heard from her sister. There's something wrong with this picture."

"Very wrong," he said. "I talked with some of the old timers. They didn't remember the car accident or the dead girl. But after I read the file and called them back, they all remembered the wife. Everybody remembers her being cool as a cucumber when she heard about it. She hardly looked at her husband and didn't shed a tear when she identified her daughter's body."

"This is so wrong," I said in disgust. I rubbed my hand over my face and leaned my elbows on the table. We looked at each other and the file for a few minutes without saying anything.

"Cops remember things like that," Uncle Glenn finally said. "It was obvious she didn't have anything to do with the wreck, but her behavior sure had the cops taking a good hard look at the possibility."

"Too bad they didn't find anything," I grunted. "Things would have been better for Libby. She might have ended up living with an uncle, but I think that would have been better than what she had."

"What are you going to do," Uncle Glenn asked. "Are you going to tell Libby?"

"No," I answered slowly. "I've already thought about it. She hasn't asked me to help. If she ever does, I'll tell her. But if she doesn't, I won't say anything."

"That's what I would do," Uncle Glenn said. "And if I ever met her mother, I'd nail her to the wall. What a piece of work that woman is."

As the tires whirred beneath them, Libby's mind went over the last day at her grandmother's. She and Sara had bounded off the bus at the end of school. The day seemed no different from many others they had shared since Libby came to Purdue Junction. The town might be a mere 168 miles from Kingsford Grove and her mother, but Libby's life was very different here with her grandmother.

Every morning on her way to the bus stop, Sara stopped at Rosemary's back door for Libby. Grumpy Mr. Stiles, the bus driver with a shaved bullet head, grunted at their happy good mornings. Classes dragged until they could to go to gym class. They ran with the track team on a route through town that had them climbing hills and sprinting blocks of straight-a-ways. Mrs. Holland, their afternoon bus driver, said hi to each of her passengers by name, assuring better behavior for her than they gave to Mr. Stiles.

That day, like every Friday, Mrs. Holland had told them to have a great weekend and not spend every minute studying. But as they approached Rosemary's cottage, Sara's mother came out the kitchen door. The girls stopped in their tracks, and then Libby ran to her."

"What's wrong?" she asked. "Where's Gram?"

"We called an ambulance to take her to the hospital," Sara's mother replied. "I brought over some groceries she asked me to get, and I found her in the garden."

"Is she okay?" Sara asked.

"I don't know," her mother replied, shaking her head and looking at Libby. "I stayed here to talk with you. And I called your uncles, Honey. Jarod will be here soon. You'll stay with us until he gets here. Why don't you go in and get clothes for tomorrow. Sara, you go with her. Bring your key, Libby. We'll make sure the house is locked up when we leave."

And just like that, her life changed again.

Now, Uncle Jarod's car headed to Kingsford Grove and Libby stared out the window without seeing anything. That day's events ran around and around in her head. Gram had waited too long for her hip replacement, probably because Diana left Libby with her. Finally one of the bones snapped and she could no longer take care of Libby. She was not coming back to her cottage in the corner of the farm where she'd raised her children. After two years, Libby was on her way back to her mother.

"What will happen to Gram's things," Libby asked without looking at her uncle.

Jarod looked over at her, surprised at the question. After going into the hospital room alone to talk with her grandmother, Libby had hardly said a word. Her uncles explained the situation to her. They thought she understood, but she'd withdrawn and they couldn't be sure. Now Jarod knew she understood everything that was going on.

"Well," he replied. "Some of it will go with her to her apartment. The family will go through the house, take what she wants to her new place, and then decide what to do with what's left. She'll help us figure things out, but that won't happen for a while. We're not going to do anything until she's had her surgery."

Libby said nothing for several miles.

"Jarod," she said suddenly, turning in her seat to face him. "Can I come back? Can I come back when you clean out the house?"

"We'll need to ask your mother," he uncle nodded as he replied. "But I don't see why not. Your mother probably won't care one way or the other. Besides, you've lived in that house for what, two years? You know what Gram has better than the rest of us, so you'd be a big help.

It will be a good way for you to say goodbye to the place and to Sara. Are there things you want?"

"Her cake things," Libby said softly.

"Her what?" Jarod asked.

"The things she uses to make cakes," Libby said. "And her knitting needles. She was teaching me. I wish I could have her garden, but I can't do that."

Jarod liked this girl. He didn't know his niece well, but what little he did know surprised him. His sister had been cold and selfish when they were growing up. Neither of the brothers had gotten close to her. This girl was friendly and funny and had helped his mother stay in her home longer that they'd thought she'd be there. He reached across the seat and touched her shoulder.

"You could have some of those seeds she always saved," he said. "You know, all those baby food jars in the pantry."

"Can I?" Libby asked eagerly. Her eyes sparkled.

"Sure," Jarod replied.

Then she slumped down in her seat again.

"What's wrong?" Jarod asked. "It sounds like a good idea to me."

"Yeah," Libby sighed, looking out the window again. "But I guess not. There won't be any place to plant them. Mom lives in an apartment."

"Have you ever heard of a Pea Patch?" Jarod said after thinking about the problem.

"No," Libby said. "What's that?"

"A Pea Patch is a lot in the city that people use for a community garden," Jarod explained. "It's a shared space that people rent so they can grow things."

"Mom wouldn't pay rent for dirt," Libby said, still deflated.

Well," Jarod replied, "I will. And your Uncle Jim will. After you get settled in with your mom, maybe you can find a Pea Patch in "hen you'd have someplace for Gram's seeds. And, maybe you can start your own.

that?" Libby asked.

"I'm not sure, but we can figure it out," he said with a grin. "You're a smart girl. You can talk to your neighbors. Talk with someone at the parks department. Maybe you can talk to the Mayor. Somebody will know what to do. I can help with that."

Libby grinned as she looked out the window. The hum of the tires lulled them back into silence. As they approached Kingsford Grove, she sat up straight and clasped her hands in her lap. She glanced at her uncle.

"She doesn't like me, you know," she said.

"Who doesn't like you?" Jarod asked.

"My Mom," Libby replied.

"It's not you," Jarod said without a pause. "It's everyone. She doesn't like anyone but the people who can help her."

He glanced at his niece. She sat rigid in her seat looking out the window. He was sure she saw nothing.

"Your Gram wouldn't like me saying this to you," he continued, "but Jim and I were surprised when we heard our sister had two daughters. We both remember that she never liked kids. Jim and I used to babysit for neighbors, but your Mom never did even though she was the girl in the family. Your Mom didn't like anything or anyone who got in the way of her thinking about herself. She always thought she was the most important thing around."

He glanced at her again. Her head seemed tilted his way so she could hear him better.

"I don't think she could help it, Libby," he said. "She was just born that way. She doesn't know there's any other way to be."

Libby said nothing. This time when he glanced at her, there were tears in her eyes.

"It's not you, Libby," he said. "Don't ever think that."

"Should I be afraid?" Libby asked as few miles later. "I mean, she hasn't ever hurt me, and I'm not afraid of her. But maybe I should be."

"I don't think you need to be afraid of her," he replied. "She's more likely to ignore you that to hurt you, don't you think?"

After thinking about it, she nodded.

"Yeah. I guess so," she said in a voice so quiet he could barely hear it.

"It's not you, Libby," he said again, matching her tone.

She turned in her seat as he stopped at a light and accelerated around the corner.

"What am I going to do, Uncle Jarod?" Libby asked. "What am I going to do now?"

"Well, I think you have two choices," he replied. "You can learn to be selfish like your Mother. Or you can use my phone number and Jim's phone number and Gram's phone number and your friends and your teachers and your neighbors to not be like your Mother. You've got lots of help out there, Libby. You just have to know when you need help and you need to ask."

"Yeah," Libby grinned a minute later as she reached across the seat and grabbed his hand. "I just have to ask."

I'm not sure why but we didn't get married. Libby wore the ring I gave her, and we kept making plans for a wedding. I was looking forward to Libby's promised groom's cake made to her grandmother's high standards and again seeing the Uncles she said we needed to invite to the ceremony. I was not looking forward to meeting her mother, but she'd be there, too. Still, we never got around to actually tying the knot. Life got busy, I guess.

I loved teaching. Libby loved working with her kids. We went to my parents' and my sister's house for parties. Bill and Maude traded dinners with us every couple of months, as did Connie and Susan. We invited each other for barbeques in the summer and chili suppers when the weather got cold. The house filled with kid sounds and laughter as we became a huge, extended family. Libby and I made a life together. I was happy.

Billy, long known as Bill, had managed a tire store for the last twelve years. Maude worked at the Kingsford Grove hospital doing billing and coding for the cancer ward. They had three stair-step boys who wore me out whenever I saw them. All the years I was single, Maude fed me on a regular basis, so I was glad to finally be able to pay her back. She was also a gardener, which gave her a bond with Libby. Whenever they were our only guests for summer suppers, Bill and I would sit on the patio talking and the two of them would walk our property looking at the plants and discussing improvements we could make.

Bill and I were still as evenly matched as we were when we were kids. But Maude and Libby were opposites who made the other look either larger or smaller than she was. I'd guess Maude to stand five feet eight or nine in her stocking feet. She was strong and solid with a broad, open face that invited you to join her in her love of life. Libby was strong and solid, too. But at full height, the top of her curly hair barely reached Maude's shoulder. That made her seem small and frail at the same time it made Maude look like an Amazon. In spite of the stares they got when they went places together, they became great friends. Many an entertaining dinner conversation centered on them mimicking people who assumed they were lesbians and all but crossed the street to avoid them.

One spring evening, Bill and Maude got a sitter and came to dinner without their boys. With a bottle of wine, plates of chicken cacciatore, and French bread with garlic butter in front of us, we shared family stories and planned our summer. Conversation paused as Maude dished up her homemade sorbet and Libby scraped plates into the sink. Bill and I watched them from the table as we enjoyed the last of the wine. Bill emptied Maude's glass into his and gave me a thumbs-up.

"Have you two ever thought about going to Mexico?" he asked.

Libby and I looked at each other and shrugged.

"We bought into a timeshare," he continued. "We're thinking about going for ten days next fall, maybe the end of September or early October. It'll depend on when Maude's mother can come to stay with the kids. The place has three bedrooms, two bathrooms, its own laundry room, and a balcony with a BBQ. Maude wants to rent a car and drive over the mountains to the heartland. If we do that we'll stay at least one night on the road. That's assuming there are motels away from the tourist meccas."

"Well," I said. "Libby does speak Spanish. I guess we have to take her along."

"Or we could take her and leave you," Maude said. She winked as she plunked a bowl in front of me.

"This is not the usual tourist place, either," Bill said. "It's not on the ocean. It's on the inside coast of the peninsula not far from the base of the Sierra Madres Mountains."

"The guide book says there are tours into the badlands where Pancho Villa holed up between raids," Maude said. "It says there are adobe walls with bullets in them. We can hike into the mountains to see parrots in their native foliage. It sounds a lot better to me than sitting in the sun on a beach with a bunch of other tourists complaining about the heat."

Bill was smiling a mysterious smile I recognized from our years as kids getting away with things we shouldn't be doing. I didn't think either of the women noticed, but I knew he had a secret.

"Are there ruins in the area?" Libby asked. "I'd love to see some of the old Indian ruins."

"Sort of," Bill replied. "The Paquine Ruins are listed but the book doesn't say much about them. That's why we'll need the car. We can drive to the ruins in less than a day. But we'll need to stay overnight someplace in order to have time to look around at those and the Pancho Villa's haunts."

"What do you think?" Libby asked me. "I'd love to go."

"Sure," I replied. "Count us in. Libby can be our interpreter."

Before they left, Libby took Maude to the office for an opinion on a new fundraiser idea. While they were out of earshot, I cornered Bill to question him on the night's mysterious smile.

"One of my great, great grandfathers lived down there," he said. "He was this charismatic guy who started his own religion. He got chased out of town after town. So he finally went to Mexico with a lot of other Americans."

"He started his own church?" I asked. I'd never thought about it, but churches had to come from someplace.

"Yup," Bill replied with a grin. "Interesting, isn't it?"

"And he took his family to Mexico," I said.

"He built a blacksmith shop in Chihuahua," Bill continued with a nod. "He made a living from that and his family kept busy running the farm that surrounded it. Mom said there's an old diary someplace that talks about getting raided by Pancho Villa and the Federalies on a regular basis. I guess there was quite an American settlement there for a while. Mom said there were several saloons and ladies of the night in town. I've always wanted to go and look around."

"So your father...what?" I asked with a scowl. "Your father took over his grandfather's church?"

"Yeah, sort of," Bill said thoughtfully. "But not exactly. Dad's religion is an off-shot of what Granddad was doing. I'll tell you about it one day, okay?"

I said sure but I never asked about it. With these new details added to what I already knew from when we were kids, I could figure it out on my own.

"This is why I hate cell phones," Libby groaned. She opened the small red rectangle and looked at the caller ID.

The friends were having lunch in a restaurant sporting round tables with red and white checked tablecloths. The food was served on red plates and the drinks in heavy red glasses. Across from Libby, Susan and Connie rolled their eyes. They knew that no matter what she said, Libby couldn't resist her phone. She always checked to see who was at the other end even if she didn't answer.

"Mom," Libby said to her friends as she got up from the table. "I'll be back before the waitress brings our food."

She headed for the hall outside the restrooms. When she returned, oversized salads sat in front of her friends and a plate of pasta was waiting for her. She took her seat, slid her phone into the purse hanging from her chair, and picked up her iced tea. Holding her glass toward the middle of the table, she gestured with her chin for her friends to do the same.

"To The Three Musketeers," she toasted. "May we go on forever."

They clinked glasses and shared a laugh before starting their food.

"So the unsinkable Diana calls again," Connie said.

"She calls me three times a day when she's unhappy," Libby said. "If things are going good, I may not hear from her for weeks. But let one thing go wrong according to Diana's rules of the world, and she calls and calls and calls. Would you believe she still asks if I've heard from Megan? After all these years, I think it's the stupidest thing she can ask."

"What does she say?" Connie frowned.

"*Have you heard from your sister,* usually," Libby sighed. "Sometimes, has *Megan called you.* She doesn't ask for details, just whether or not Meg has called."

The heads across from her shook in unison.

"How many times have you explained that Megan isn't coming back?" Susan asked.

"Too many to count," Libby replied. "My two cents' worth is that she understands that Megan is gone. But she won't let her brain or her heart accept it. If she did that, she might actually understand that she was at fault. I'm willing to bet we'll be having this same conversation when I'm sixty."

"I've said before that I'd be crazy if my mother called as often as yours does," Susan said, shaking her head.

"I don't know how you stand it," Connie put in. "She's always been one of the most selfish people I've met. You call her an eccentric. I call her an egomaniac."

"Right," Susan put in. "It's just mean for her to ask about Megan."

"Well, she did her best," Libby replied with a sigh. "Dad taking Meg hurt me. But it did something to her, too. I could be mad about what she does, but it would be a waste of time. And remember that when I came back from Gram's she really did try to do better."

"What else did she have to say?" Susan asked.

"Once again, she called to complain about Al," Libby said. "Right now she's living in a two thousand square foot, third floor condo in gorgeous Boston, for heaven's sake. And I like this guy. My two cents' worth is that she should be happy with what she's got, but I've decided that's never to happen. She's going to be unhappy until she runs out of men and is living in a nursing home gumming her food."

"How many does this make?" Susan asked. "Six?'

"More like eight," Connie laughed as she held a fork filled with lettuce halfway between the plate and her mouth.

"Actually," Libby said slowly, drawing out each syllable. "I'd have to count, but he might be number eleven or twelve. Would you believe she doesn't use Al's name when she talks about him? She calls him her *current husband*."

Connie and Susan laughed.

"Remember that one guy when we were in high school?" Susan said. "The one with the really thick glasses and brown hair that stuck out like straw all the time."

"My favorite was the short guy," Connie said. "You remember. The top of his head came to about the middle of her neck. Whenever I saw them together, I wondered how they kissed. Not that I knew much about kissing back then, but I couldn't figure out how they managed it. Even now it seems odd."

"I remember he wore black suits," Susan put in. "He was wearing a black suit every time I saw him. Remember the Fourth of July that year? He barbequed hot dogs wearing a black suit."

"He was a nice guy, though," Libby smiled at the memory. "He didn't take much crap from Mom. I think he was the first guy who tried to get her thinking about the future. He actually wanted her to make plans further ahead than next Saturday. That might be why she got rid of him."

"Which one did you like the best?" Connie asked.

Libby thought about the question for a minute while she ate a few bites of pasta.

"There were two I hoped she would marry," she said. "Remember when we were seniors and Mom came home with the guy in kakis and a blue polo shirt? Remember how she said she was drinking coffee outside the golf store at the mall and this guy asked if he could share her table since she was alone and the other tables were full? He always wore polo shirts. I think he had one in every color of the rainbow."

Her friends nodded.

"My two cents' worth is that he was one of the good guys," Libby said. "I'm pretty sure they didn't sleep together in our apartment the whole time they dated. That had to be his idea because Mom wasn't too concerned about me. He bought groceries and fixed stuff around the apartment. He gave me money for school events and was gentle with Mom right up to the day she sent him packing. I always thought he'd make a good stepfather if I was going to have one."

"Was he the one who dubbed us The Three Musketeers?" Susan asked.

"He was," Connie said. "Remember he drove us to the movies while Diana got ready to out to dinner? We were dressed the same and we finished each other's sentences, so he called us The Three Musketeers."

"Are you sure?" Susan asked. "I remember that happening, but I'm not sure he was the one who drove us."

"Trust me," Connie said. "It was Mr. Polo shirt. I remember his shirt was pink that night because it matched our shorts."

"Who else did you want her to keep?" Susan asked Libby.

"The other guy I really wanted her to marry and keep around was Armando," Libby continued slowly, a grin on her face. "My two cent's worth is that he was the best guy she ever dated. I actually thought they might stay together."

"Armando," Connie said dreamily.

"His hair was so shiny," Susan said as she sighed and touched her chest. "It was perfect and it always looked like he'd just come from the barber's. He smelled *so* good."

"He was around longer than the others, wasn't he?" Connie asked.

"I don't know for sure," Libby replied. "But it seems like he was. That might be because I liked him and he paid more attention to me than most of the others. And not the creepy attention like some of them gave me. Armando treated me like an adult even if I was only fourteen or fifteen at the time. If he stayed over, he was always up before I went to school."

"He stayed over?" Connie said with a grin. "Surprise, surprise."

"Hardly," Susan put in. "I don't know how anyone could keep their hands off him."

"Well, he'd sit at the table with me while I ate breakfast even if he just had coffee," Libby said. "He signed Mom's name to a couple of field trip forms when she forgot and I couldn't get her out of bed to do it. And he taught me some Spanish so I could express my frustration with Mom. We had so much fun she got mad and forbade me to speak anything but English when she was in the room. After she got rid of him, I decided to learn Spanish. You guys know that. Anyway, those are the two I really hoped would stay around. But she didn't start marrying them until I was out of the house. I guess we have to give her credit for that."

"Remember the guy with suspenders," Susan laughed. "Red suspenders. Blue suspenders. Suspenders with bugs on them. I thought he was a strange one."

"So who is her current husband?" Connie asked. "What does he do?"

"His name is Allen Ross. And he doesn't do anything, as far as I know," Libby replied. "I think he's a retired travel agent. Well, not a travel agent. If I don't have him confused with someone else, he used to own travel agencies in the northeast and he sold them when he retired. He can keep Mom in the fashion she wants to be kept in and doesn't seem to mind doing it."

"What's she complaining about?" Connie asked.

"Today it's the way he folded the paper after he read it," Libby replied. "Yesterday it was that he left his socks and boxers *on* the hamper instead of putting them *in* the hamper. Last week she called to let me know he dunked his toast in his egg yolk at breakfast and she didn't know how to tell him she hated it."

"So there's nothing wrong with him," Susan said. "Just like old times."

"Just like old times," Libby said. "Can we talk about something else? Something more interesting than my mother's love life?"

"Okay," Connie said. "I have gossip."

The day of Uncle Glenn's birthday celebration, Libby arrived at the Moran's with a decorated half-sheet cake from the grocery store. Setting the box on the kitchen counter, she lifted the lid and asked for help to move the cake to the table. Tanner's mother balanced one end and they took the cake out of the box.

"This is wonderful," Mrs. Moran commented. She swiped a finger full of frosting and put it in her mouth. "Tanner loves frosting flowers. He can eat that corner with the roses, and he'll be a kid on a sugar high."

"Do you really have beans and wieners for his birthday dinner?" Libby asked.

"Yes," his mother replied. "He's asked for that since he was about seven years old. I've modified it many times, but it's still basically beans and wieners. These days I use three kinds of beans and Polish sausage, but nobody can say I don't honor his request."

"What did Uncle Glenn order?" Libby asked.

"Glenn is a chicken man," Mrs. Moran smiled. "He prefers fried, but he'll eat baked. He has to have mashed potatoes swimming in gravy. And he needs cranberry dressing on the side. I'm sure that's something their mother did when they were kids."

"I brought meatloaf," Libby said. "I didn't know what you were making, but I thought everyone likes meatloaf."

"It will get eaten," Mrs. Moran replied. "We can put it in the oven with the rest of the stuff to stay warm."

Libby went to her car and returned with a gift in one hand and the pan of meatloaf in the other. They slid the pan into the oven and then took the gift to the dining room. Libby laughed when she saw the stack of wrapped boxes heaped in the middle of the table.

"My two cents' worth is that this is far too many gifts for a man his age," she said. "This looks like a kid's birthday party."

"Oh, don't be fooled," Mrs. Moran said. "It looks impressive, but I know good and well some of those boxes contain a single sock. Randall is well known for separating pairs of things and wrapping them in different boxes."

"He must be fun at Christmastime," Libby replied.

"The year he had money from his first job, he gave me new kitchen utensils," Tanner's mother said with a fond smile as she looked at the pile of gifts. "I had a couple dozen pretty boxes of every shape and size under the tree. One was a spatula, one was a knife, and another was an old-fashioned eggbeater. He put potholders in tubes and wrapped them like those party favors you buy for New Year's Eve. Yes, our Randall enjoys himself on birthdays and Christmas."

Libby laughed.

"Thanks for bringing the cake," Mrs. Moran continued. "There are so many of us now that we need two cakes just so everyone get a piece. Maude is bringing a chocolate cake and Marta is in charge of the ice cream."

"What else can I help with," Libby asked.

Hours later, kids were playing in the yard while the adults watched them through the dining room window. Glasses filled with wine and beer sat on a table littered with wrapping paper. There was a stack of gifts in front of Uncle Glenn, who was leaning back in his chair with a silly grin on his face. Libby smiled just watching him.

After opening all the packages, he had proclaimed Marta's gift the best of the day. Tucked in a box with a squirt gun, she had given him a gray tie decorated with what at first looked like black squares. A closer inspection showed that the squares were tiny handgun illustrations.

"You can bury me in this one," he said as he gave Marta a hug. "Put it on me with my gray suit when you put me in the ground."

"Okay," Marta replied. "I'll be sure to remember that request. You just make sure it's not for a long time, okay?"

"A very long time," Tanner said.

"Billy....opps, sorry," Randall said to his brother. "Bill says you're planning a Mexican vacation next fall."

"We're talking about a non-resort town," Tanner replied. "And a two-day road trip into the mountains to see some of the old Indian ruins."

"We're going to head to Chihuahua," Bill said. "I had a grandfather who lived down there after the Civil War. I want to look around and see if I'm missing any family heritage."

"What was he doing down there?" Marta asked.

"He got chased out of the states because some of his fellow citizens didn't like his religion," Bill said.

"What religion was that?" Mr. Moran asked.

"His own," Bill laughed and held up his hands to fend off more questions. "He started his own church."

The others looked at one another without comment as they waited to see what Bill would say next.

"I hear he was an ornery guy, but he did okay down there," he continued. "He church flourished as other Americans migrated. He was a blacksmith and while his wives and kids farmed to keep them fed, he kept both the Federalies and Pancho Villa's men in horseshoes.

Supposedly, both sides would swoop into their compound, demand food, and then enjoy themselves drinking too much while Granddad took care of their horses."

"Do you think the stories are true?" Uncle Glenn asked.

"I think so," Bill replied. "Tanner and I found some newspaper clippings and old photographs in the attic when we were kids. There were also some interesting tools in the shed. We couldn't figure out what they were until we found the newspaper articles. I'm sure most of the tools were Granddad's. I don't know how Dad got them. He never talked about it and I sure never saw him use them."

"The coolest one was a bellows," Tanner put in. "We figured he must have needed to get the fire really hot really fast, and he did that by aiming the bellows where he wanted it and using his foot to control the air aimed at the coals. We….ah….tried it one winter."

"What?" his father said. "You boys built a fire in that old shed?"

"Hey! You promised not to tell!" Bill exclaimed, punching Tanner's shoulder.

"Yeah," Tanner replied as he tried to move away. "Sorry about that."

"Anyway, our condo is a little ways in from the coast," Maude said. "We plan to drive to Chihuahua, find a motel, visit the ruins and Bill's grandfather's land early the next day, and drive back to the motel after we look around. We might need a second day, but I doubt it."

"How are you going to navigate," Marta asked. "I don't believe you speak Spanish."

"No," Bill and Tanner said at the same time.

"But Libby does," Maude put in with bravado.

All eyes turned to Libby.

"One of my mother's boyfriends spoke Spanish," she said. "He taught me a few phrases, and I got interested in the idea of knowing more than one language. I took classes in high school and college.

My two cents' worth is that I probably know just enough to keep us out of trouble."

"*One* of you mother's boyfriends?" Marta laughed. "How many did she have?"

Libby looked uncomfortable. She glanced at Tanner for help.

"Don't ask her that," Tanner said, holding both hands in front of his face in a panic gesture. "I think it was an even dozen the last time I heard. If you get her started, we'll be here all night. Who wants more cake?"

Libby made the house into a home without much help from me. My job at the academy took more time than I'd expected. I loved teaching. I loved taking a suggestion and building it into a class. I loved standing in front of a group, doing my thing, and seeing the light come on in their eyes. I loved answering questions with stories from my days on the street. For the first time since I started with the police department, I felt like I was actually contributing, actually making a difference. I had experience from more than twenty years on the job, and I was able to pass that on to the newbies. It felt good.

For the first eight months, I drove to the academy early Sunday morning and stayed until the end of the last class on Thursday. I got home after eleven Thursday night, spent Friday and Saturday with Libby, and headed back on Sunday. I'd been assured that once I had my classes planned out and some teaching experience under my belt, I wouldn't need to spend as much time away from home. I hoped this was true because I wanted more time with Libby.

Between my weekend visits, Libby spent her time transforming the house. After I signed the paperwork and got the keys, we moved in some furniture from my apartment and some from hers. The rest we took to the Goodwill. Our plan was to buy new things as we had the money and Libby had the ideas.

The house had two bedrooms on the main floor along with the living room, kitchen, and a large bathroom. Libby painted one bedroom mint green and put white wainscoting on three walls. Then one weekend she hauled me to the store to buy a new bed and find linens we could both live with. I was dreading the lace and flowers I thought we'd end up with since she had a bright flowered sofa when I first met her. But that wasn't what Libby had in mind. She showed me three comforters that didn't sport a single flower. I picked one with a geometric design in greens and chocolate brown. Libby matched it with soft brown sheets, two oversized round pillows I use when I read in bed, and brown accessories for the bathroom.

Now our king size bed is angled across one corner of the room. There's a wide bench at the bottom of the bed and black-and-white movie posters of manly movies like *12 Angry Men, 400 Blows,* and *On the Waterfront* displayed on the walls above the wainscoting. There's a bookcase holding the television and our combined collection of movies. A tall chest of drawers I got from my parents when I moved into my first apartment is tucked into the corner by the closet.

The living room and kitchen she painted a glossy off-white and accented with primary colors. She recovered her comfy flowered sofa in a nubby, mustard-colored fabric and the pillows in blue, red, and green. Two new mustard gingham chairs with plain pillows face the living room side of the fireplace. The recliner from my old place is now a blue that shouldn't look good in the room. But it fits right in. Fleece throws are draped everywhere and get used a lot during the winter.

Our kitchen sports chickens of all sorts in black and white with the same primary color accents as the living room. A rooster with beady eyes and a bold red comb lords it over the table from a poster on the wall. Black and white chicken-shaped salt-and-pepper shakers regularly migrate from the back of the stove to the table and back again.

Libby turned the other bedroom on the main floor into an office. We have small desks facing each other near the window, two computers, and a printer that's newer than the one I use at work. The off-white walls display a mishmash of our personal stuff, from family pictures to awards. She's put two more of the mustard colored chairs in the corner facing the office side of the fireplace. I suspect that corner is where she spends a lot of time when I'm not home.

As far as I can tell, except for one utility light and a dark bamboo shade on the big window, she didn't do anything to improve the basement. She slowly bought what she needed to work in the yard and a lot of that got stored downstairs. A green wheelbarrow was leaning against the wall beside the door one weekend when I got home. A hoe, shovel and rake were shiny new on pegs the next. Then hoses and electrical cords found their way into our life.

One weekend I looked around when I got home and didn't see any changes. When I asked her about her week, she walked me through the basement and across the yard, grinning the whole time. She'd bought a pair of composting bins, set them up under the apple trees, and proudly showed me how they worked. I would never have guessed that composting bins would make her happy. Who knew she was so easy to please?

True to her word, Libby did all the planning and most of the work. I was happy about that, but I helped when she told me what to do.

On a cool Saturday morning as we finished breakfast, Libby jumped at the sound of a vehicle on the gravel out front.

"I forgot he was coming," she said as she headed for the stairs. "I need to move the lawnmower. Have him drive around back."

I found a man in a small flatbed truck waiting for me in front of the house. Strapped to the truck bed was a large rectangular table.

He carefully backed down the slope to where Libby stood. I helped him unload the heavy, scarred table and jiggle it two-legs-at-a-time through the door and into the basement. Our last maneuver at Libby's direction placed it in front of the window and under the newly installed light.

After refusing a cup of coffee, the man drove back up the slope, crunched across the gravel, and disappeared down the street.

Libby smiled at me.

"I'll use this for bedding plants in the spring," she said, pleased as punch with her find.

"Okay," I said, raising my eyebrows at her delight.

I wasn't sure what she was talking about. Until Randall and I were grown, my family had lived in rental houses where the only upkeep we did was take care of the lawn. If my mother planted flowers, they came from displays at the grocery store.

One spring weekend I came home to find little square pots of dirt warming under the utility light. After dinner, Libby dragged me to the basement and gave me paper packets of seeds. We poked holes in the soil of each pot, dropped in seeds, and pushed soil back over them. In a couple of weeks, they sprouted little green heads. A while after that, I helped her move the plants to larger pots, then a few weeks after that we moved them to even larger ones. By the time it warmed up outside, the table was filled with flowers ready for the porch and vegetables ready for the garden.

"How do you know how to do this?" I asked as we carried planters outside.

"My grandmother," Libby smiled. "I lived with her for two years after Dad and Megan left. Gram was a wonderful, gentle woman who liked to teach anyone who would listen. I was a captive audience so she shared all sorts of things, including what she knew about gardening. I thought it was too much work back then. But as I got older, I knew she'd given me a gift."

She had apparently learned a lot from this grandmother I knew little about. As she plied that knowledge in our yard, I came to realize that she hadn't lied when she said her time working in the dirt was her therapy. She still didn't talk to me much about the abused kids she saw or the bureaucratic knots she had to untie to get them the help they needed. Instead, her anger went into digging in the garden or trimming the trees.

Slowly, the yard began to emerge from the overgrown acres I bought with the house. She built a sturdy replacement for the fence in the back yard. She dug a flowerbed under the short fence and filled it with pink and purple flowers. She made an interesting and simple patio by nailing lengths of two-by-fours into squares and setting them into the ground on both sides of the fence. She found a small table with chairs and two canvas lounge chairs to make the space usable. My assignment was to find the grill I wanted and set it up on the patio.

Along the side of the house from the gravel drive out front to her patio, she built a walkway of broken cement chunks so large I wondered how she moved them. Between the cement she planted some sort of low growing plants that made the walk to the backyard welcoming. More pink and purple flowers grew between the house and the walk and in the two planters on the front steps.

The first year we lived in the house, I'd start guessing what work she'd done as I drove home from the academy. At first, it wasn't too hard because she was working inside. Paint was a good guess when we first moved in. Then, for a while, furniture changes were obviously in the works because she asked me about colors and what kind of chairs I liked. But after that, it was hard to know what she'd be doing while I was gone. The changes were always a surprise. And every one of them made the house more and more a home.

Libby pulled her car past the porch and backed up until her trunk was close to the steps. After unlocking the front door, she unloaded a quart of paint, sandpaper, two brushes, and a painter's tarp. Then she moved her car to its usual parking spot.

As she climbed the porch stairs, she pulled her ringing cell phone from her pocket.

"Hello," she said without checking the caller ID.

"Elizabeth, it's your mother."

"Hi, Mom," Libby replied. She walked through the house to the kitchen where she dampened a dishcloth and opened a drawer.

"Do you remember when you were little and you spent that summer with your grandmother," her mother asked.

"Well, I wasn't so little," Libby replied. She found a screwdriver, picked up the dishcloth, and went back to the front door. "I was eleven. And it wasn't a summer. Remember I went to live with her after Dad and Megan left? I lived with Gram for two years."

Shortly after her Uncle Jarod took her back to her mother, she had taken his advice: she asked for help. She'd been living with Diana for three months when her mother began asking her if she'd seen her sister at school. Spooked and afraid her mother was having some sort of breakdown, she called her uncle. Jarod called her school and arranged for her to talk with the school psychologist.

The woman listened well and gave Libby a few skills to help handle her mother. Among other things, she convinced Libby that one of the most important things for her to do was to be truthful with Diana no matter what she said or did. There was a danger that Libby would begin to believe the lies if she started agreeing with her mother to make her happy. And lying to her mother wouldn't solve anything. Beginning that day, Libby was factual with Diana and she learned to keep her emotions out of any references her mother made to Megan.

"I guess that's right," her mother said. "I don't remember anymore. By the way, have you heard from your sister?"

"Nope," Libby replied with the usual eye roll to the ceiling. "I doubt if I ever will."

Her mother said nothing. The phone line was silent as Libby tested the screwdriver in a screw holding one of the dragon doorknockers in place.

"Mom?" she asked loudly when Diana didn't continue.

"I'm here," was the reply.

"Why are you calling," Libby asked. With the phone tucked awkwardly between her chin and shoulder, she turned the screwdriver with one hand and held a dragon firm with the other.

"What?" her mother asked.

"Why are you calling?" Libby asked back. "What about Gram. What do you want to know?"

"Oh, that's right," her mother said. "I need to know if she taught you anything about houseplants."

"Houseplants," Libby said thoughtfully. "Well, Gram had plenty of them. She had a line of African violets on both windowsills in the kitchen and those vine things in most of the other rooms. She gave me a spider plant for my room that I gave to Sara when I left. But I don't remember her teaching me anything about them. Why?"

"My current husband says I need some houseplants," her mother replied. "I don't want something I need to take care of."

"What kind of plants?" Libby asked.

"I think he said fig trees," Diana replied.

"Why would Al want you to have houseplants? Libby asked.

"He says they'd brighten up the condo and maybe give me something to do."

"My two cents' worth is that houseplants aren't really a hobby, Mom," Libby replied as she removed another dragon from the door.

"I think maybe you water them once a week. Your cleaning lady could probably do that for you when she comes in."

"Do you think so?" her mother asked. Her voice brightened.

"Sure," Libby replied. "If you wanted to make it a hobby, you could attend lectures or volunteer at city parks."

"I guess I could do the lectures," her mother said slowly, seeming to think about Libby's suggestion. "But not the parks. I don't like to get dirty. I would not do that even to make my current husband happy."

Libby laughed. How well she knew this about her mother.

"I know," she said. "What was Al thinking?"

With one hand she awkwardly unfolded the drop cloth and slid it under the open door so it covered both the porch and the floor of the front hall. She placed the three dragon doorknockers inside on the floor and pushed the door open far enough that it stopped snug against them.

"I don't know," her mother replied. "I never know what that man is thinking. He always wants me to do something I don't want to do."

Libby lightly sanded the door while she talked. When she'd sanded top to bottom, she wiped away the sawdust. Then she moved the paint can to the drop cloth and used the screwdriver to open it. She dipped a brush into the deep blue liquid.

"Maybe he thinks you're bored," Libby said.

She knew this was true. Al had asked her how he could get his wife interested in something besides shopping and lunch with her friends. He had many ideas, but Libby knew most of them wouldn't make any difference. All these and more had been tried by Libby and the men who came before Al, her mother's current adoring husband.

"Well, I'm not," her mother said fiercely. Libby imagined Diana standing straighter and squaring her shoulders for an argument. "I'm as fine as I can be. You know I've never been bored in my life."

"Somehow, you need to let Al know that," Libby replied. "He worries about you. He's a good guy, Mom. He cares about you."

"Oh, I guess," her mother sighed. "I'll let you go. Say hello to your sister for me when she calls, okay?"

Libby set the phone on the porch railing. She painted the door carefully from top to bottom. When it was finished, she stood back to look at it. Without the dragons, the door seemed a bit naked. But she liked the blue. She liked it a lot. And it would be even better when the dragons went back up.

As advertised, the condo in Navajoa, Mexico, was large and comfortable. They landed in Guaymas late morning, rented a car, and drove south with the gulf disappearing in the rearview mirror. The short drive was interrupted twice. Once by a stop for groceries and once by a photo op in front of a spectacularly deformed pine tree where they bought lunch from a gray-haired man whose taco truck was parked nearby.

When the groceries and their clothes were unpacked, the four of them went to the pool. Two women sat talking in lounge chairs under green and white umbrellas, and a thin man in a tiny Speedo practiced his dives. After a short swim, Libby joined Maude under an umbrella while Tanner and Bill swam laps on opposite sides of the pool. Finally, they retired to the condo for showers and naps.

The next day was spent exploring Navojoa. Although the town didn't exist solely for tourists, it was obvious that Americans and other visitors still found their way this far south. Twice they crossed paths with a Japanese tour group decked out in shorts and cameras. A wiry American in a souvenir shop sold them a map, along with advice, a five-gallon gas can, and an air pump with metal foot pedal. He also put bold red X's on the map to show the only three gas stations on the road over the mountains.

The second morning was an early one. While Tanner and Maude made sandwiches for the road, Bill spread a map on the kitchen table. They would head north back through Guaymas to Hermosilla and then take Highway 16 across the mountains. The old man had assured them they'd find two small but adequate motels in Chihuahua.

As Tanner packed their lunch and Maude put a skillet on the stove to start breakfast, Libby came into the kitchen. She was pale. Her hair stuck out every which way. And she was still in her sleep shirt.

"I think you're going without me," she said in an exhausted voice. "I feel awful."

Tanner and Bill looked up. Maude stepped to Libby and put her hands on her forehead.

"You're burning up," she said.

"Yeah, but I'm freezing," Libby replied with a shudder. "And I have a headache that could split wood. I can't find my Advil. Did any of you bring something I can take?"

Bill headed to the bedroom and came back with a bottle of Advil. He also gave her a large bottle of Pepto Bismol.

"How did you know?" she tried to joke as she took the bottle.

"You've got the look," he said. "You've got that green around the gills look Tanner used to get when we partied hardy and he was going to barf."

Libby gave him a weak chuckle and looked at Tanner.

"I'm going back to bed," she said. "You guys go to Chihuahua and bring me back some postcards so I can say I was there."

Bill, Maude and Tanner exchanged a look. Libby found a bottle of water in the refrigerator and took two pills.

"We can put this off until you feel better," Tanner said. "We don't have to go today."

"I know," Libby replied. "But if you do that we'll have to bump everything else we have planned. Besides, how much rest do you think

I'd get with you hovering around and checking on me every few minutes? Go. I'll sleep and I'll be okay."

"I can stay with her," Tanner said, looking from Maude to Bill. "You two go and bring us pictures."

"No," Libby said firmly. "Eat your breakfast, check on me before you leave, and then check on me when you get back."

"She's right," Maude said. "She needs sleep. She can do that better without the three of us tiptoeing around trying to be quiet."

Reluctantly, Tanner opened the refrigerator and took out six bottles of water. Maude found a box of crackers in a grocery bag and handled it to him. Then he walked Libby back to their bedroom.

"You're sure about this?" he asked as he tucked her under the blankets. He put the bottled water and crackers on the nightstand within easy reach. "I can stay."

"I'm sure," she said with a small smile as she snuggled under the blankets. "There are other things on the itinerary I can do when I feel better. Go. Have fun. Bring me a post card."

"I'm going," he said. He kissed her forehead. "Wow. You really are burning up."

Libby dozed for a while with voices floating to her from the kitchen. Then she woke up enough to hear the door of the condo close and voices fade down the hall. She turned on her side and closed her eyes again.

Three gallon jars sat on the steps to Gram's kitchen. Six tea bags, secured under the lid by their tags, dangled into the brown water in each jar. Libby, twelve years old again and home after her day at school, waved to Sara and walked past the jars and into the kitchen.

Gram's house smelled like sugar. Three square pans were cooling on the counter and a spool of heavy black button thread sat beside them.

"Gram," Libby called at the top of her lungs.

"In here."

Libby dropped her schoolbooks on the table and followed her grandmother's voice. Gram, Uncle Jim, and Uncle Jarod sat in the living room. They smiled at her.

"Come here, Dear," Gram said.

Libby obediently went across the room and sat on the floor between her grandmother's knees. With her favorite brush, Rosemary began brushing Libby's hair. She separated it into small sections and braided it in one long braid down her back.

"Doesn't she have great hair?" Rosemary asked.

"Yup," Uncle Jim said.

"Yup," Uncle Jarod echoed.

Gram unbraided the hair and brushed it again. She twisted it tight against Libby's head and secured it with her shortest knitting needle.

"When I'm gone, I want her to have all my sewing things," Gram said. "You boys remember that."

"Okay," Uncle Jarod said.

"Okay," Uncle Jim echoed.

Libby said nothing. Her uncles smiled at her.

"Come on to the kitchen," Gram said. "That tea should be ready by now. You need a drink, don't you?"

"Sure," Uncle Jim said.

"Sure," Uncle Jarod echoed.

As they passed Libby on their way to the kitchen, each uncle smiled at her and gripped the top of her head with strong fingers, giving it a squeeze.

Libby followed them to the kitchen, but when they walked through the door, they disappeared. Suddenly only Gram was there. She held out the spool of thread to Libby.

"I'm going to show you how to make two layers out of one cake, okay?" she asked.

Libby reached for the thread.

Libby opened her eyes. After figuring out where she was, she sat up and reach for a bottle of water. Her head was throbbing worse than ever but a glance at the clock said she'd only been asleep a few minutes. She put her head back down on the pillow and her hands on her hot forehead. Tears ran down her temples. She shivered, turned over, and closed her eyes,

Rosemary reached around Libby and showed her how to hold the rosette tool and move it in her fingers. A young Libby repeated the action until she was able to rotate it easily.

Using a bag of frosting, Rosemary made a perfect rose. She gave Libby the bag and watched as her granddaughter tried unsuccessfully to squeeze frosting from it while she maneuvered the stem in her other hand. After eating a dab of frosting that had fallen on the table, Rosemary demonstrated again and handed the bag back to Libby. The teenaged Libby tried and failed to make more roses.

Morphing instantly into a grown Libby, she was deftly making frosting roses and setting them one after the other on waxed paper to set up. In her own kitchen, she spread thick chocolate frosting on two layers of chocolate cake. Then she began moving frosting roses from the waxed paper to the top of the cake.

Tanner came into the kitchen wearing only boxers and hair flat from sleep. He reached around her, swiped a rose with his index finger, and put it in his mouth.

"Two chocolate cakes?" he asked.

"One for you and one for Bill," she answered.

"He always gets a white cake," Tanner said in a pouty little-boy voice. "I get chocolate and he gets white. That's the rule."

"Not this year," Libby said.

Her headache woke her again. The clock said she'd been asleep for ten minutes. She rolled onto her back and stared at the ceiling. Trying to forget the pain in her head so she could sleep, she thought about

The Bertram House and the children she'd loved through the years. She thought she would never get to sleep. She thought her head would never feel better. She closed her eyes and started to count backwards from one hundred.

Eight identical boxes sat on the counter in BB's kitchen. Teams of children who shared a bedroom were handed a box and told to take it to their room and then go to the rec room on the third floor. Libby and Sam took the last box upstairs and waited until everyone was there. With a flourish, Sam opened the box and held out its contents.

"Tell me what this is," he said to the roomful of kids.

"A pretend ladder," one of the boys shouted.

All the children laughed. Libby stood at the back of the room watching everyone.

"Pretend?" Sam shouted back as he grinned at them. "It's not pretend. It's a window ladder. You use it to get out of your room if there's a fire. We're going to teach you how to use it so you'll be safe. Ready?"

"Ready!" the children shouted.

While Sam fixed the ladder on the windowsill and unrolled it down the outside of the house, Libby watched the children. Fear, interest, and humor played on their faces as they took in the information and absorbed their new responsibility of helping each other if the house caught fire.

Hannah, her first child, stood with her arms tight across her chest. She was afraid, as usual. Rick with the big smile jumped up and down in place so he could see what was going on by the window. The three Roberts stood together though they'd been at BB's at different times. Colleen, who came to them with two broken arms, stood alone at one side of the group watching cautiously before taking her place in line.

One by one, her kids took a turn adjusting the ladder to be sure it was snug. One by one, under Sam's direction, her kids crawled out the window and disappeared into the darkness.

When only she and Sam were left, he turned and held his hand out to her.

"Your turn, Libby" he said. "You need to know how to do this, too. You never know, one day, you might be the only one who can save somebody."

This time when she opened her eyes, her whole body was burning up. She was sure her fever was worse. The clock said it was still too soon for more Advil since she'd only been asleep another ten minutes. She rolled onto her stomach, tucked her hands under her thighs, and closed her eyes.

She was chasing Meg. They ran around the house and Meg went through the hedge to the Ferrall's yard. Libby followed her and almost caught Meg's arm as she went down the driveway between the Ferrall's cars. They ran back to their own yard, around the house once, and then up the stairs and into the kitchen. Meg took a knife from the wooden block.

"Here," she said, trying to give Libby the knife. "Kill me. Kill me now."

Libby backed away from Meg until she bumped into the counter. Behind her sister, their father came in the door. He stood looking at them with a big smile on his face. Libby smiled at him and Meg turned to see who was behind her. As soon as he had their attention, their father's smile turned into a wide, toothless grin. Meg dropped the knife and moved closer to Libby.

"Come with me," he said. "I have a new place for you to live."

"We can't," Libby said.

"Mom said you can't come in the house," Meg said.

"It's my house," he roared in a voice that wasn't his.

In a burst of flames, their father turned red and grew a tail and pointed ears. He reached big hands with long, black fingernails toward the girls.

"Run," Libby shouted. "Run, Meg!"

Libby took Meg's hand and started to run through the house.

"No!" Meg said and dug in her heels. "We have to stay with Daddy."

Libby didn't look back. She ran out the front door, across the yard, through the hedge, and finally crouched between the cars in the Ferrell's driveway. When she looked back, the red devil flew out the kitchen door and off into the sky. He pointed a long fingernail at Libby and smiled, his sharp teeth showing in his black mouth. Megan was tucked under his arm. Libby screamed.

Libby jerked awake and look around the room in confusion. Her head was still splitting and was hot to her touch. She got out of bed and went to the bathroom. She rummaged in Tanner's shaving kit without finding what she was looking for. In the other bathroom she looked first in Bill's shaving kit and then Maude's makeup bag. Finally she found a bottle of Tylenol PM. She took three tablets and went to the kitchen.

She found a spoon in the kitchen drawer and swallowed some Pepto Bismol. She took the Tylenol PM tablets even though it was still too soon and three tablets were too many to take at one time. She paused at the window to look down at the pool. The same two women were under the stripped umbrellas. The same man in the Speedos was practicing his dives. Three teenaged boys were rough-housing in the water though she couldn't hear the splashes or their voices from where she was.

Holding her head with one hand, she made her way back to bed. She took off her sleep shirt and got under the blanket. She lay on her side with one knee drawn up and the blanket pulled tight against her neck. She was still burning up, still sick to her stomach. She needed to get some sleep. She started counting backwards again.

She was in Tanner's kitchen. She filled a tall glass at the sink and drank it down. She filled it again, drank it down again. When she turned around, the rooster with the red comb was gone from his place in the poster.

She looked under the table. She opened each kitchen cupboard and bent over to look inside. The rooster wasn't there. He was hiding and she had to find him. She had to get him back into the poster before Tanner saw that he was loose in the house. What a mess she'd have to clean up when she got the bird back where he belonged.

As she started through the house she'd lovingly decorated, she walked from their kitchen into Gram's living room. She grabbed a knitting needle in each hand and cautiously walked down the hall. There was a sharp pain in her right ankle. She looked down and saw blood.

The rooster was running at her legs, pecking holes in her skin. She tried to shoo him away with the knitting needles. The rooster shook his blood-red comb at her, grabbed one of the needles in his beak, and took it away from her. She ran.

In her Grandmother's bedroom, she dived onto the bed and pulled the blankets over her head. She felt the rooster land on her chest, furiously pecking at the blankets. She cried out and held the blankets tight to the mattress so he couldn't get to her.

Then she felt a familiar heavy weight land near her feet. The rooster squawked, and she heard him fly away. The weight walked up her body and sat on her chest where the rooster had perched to peck at her. She lowered the blankets far enough to peek out. She saw Big Boy sitting on her. She saw green walls and white wainscoting. She saw familiar movie posters. She was in Tanner's big bed where she belonged. Big Boy nosed her nose and licked her cheek with a rough tongue. He circled her head twice, nudging her as he found his spot, and then curled up with his rump next to her ear. The deep purr vibrating in his chest played a comforting lullaby.

Libby slept.

Snow was forecast for the weekend. I expected the storm to come in as I drove toward home, but I made it to the house before anything started falling from the dark clouds. When I pushed the door open, the house was filled with the aroma of cinnamon and beef. In the kitchen, a crockpot steamed on the counter beside empty bowls and a plate filled with cookies. The table was set with silverware and glasses. I grabbed a spoon, lifted the lid, and stole a spoonful of something brown and bubbly. Libby's beef stew. It was heavenly. I resisted the cookies.

In the bedroom I changed clothes and emptied my suitcase. As I pulled a sweatshirt over my head, movement in the backyard caught my eye. I went to the window to see what Libby was working on today.

The clippers she held looked too big for her. She was standing in an apple tree with one foot anchored in the V of branches below her and the other leg braced against the trunk. I could see her favorite red-handled saw hooked on a branch. She reached as high as she could with the clippers and clamped them around a limb. As I watched, she used every muscle in her body to tighten the teeth and clip off the limb. Once it fell to the ground, she climbed higher and started on a larger branch with the saw.

I went out to see if she needed my help.

"Hey," I called as I sat down to tie on my boots.

She looked my way and smiled. By the time I got to the tree, the clippers and saw leaned against the trunk. She'd climbed down and was dragging a limb toward a pile of limbs she'd already moved to the back of the lot near the property line.

"I thought you were waiting until spring to trim these," I said.

"That was my plan," Libby replied. "But I couldn't stay inside. You know how it is."

I didn't know. A storm was coming and the air was cold on my face. I'd been happy in an apartment with no trees to take care of. But

I nodded and followed her, dragging the other limb. The pile was substantial. I could tell she'd been at it for a while.

"Are you building a bonfire?" I asked as we walked back to the trees.

"Nope," she smiled. "We're going to turn all this into firewood. Next weekend, you're going to help me split and stack it. We won't be able to burn it this year. But my two cents' worth is that it'll be dry enough for us to use next winter."

"Hmmm," I raised my eyebrows at her and she laughed.

She picked up the clippers and saw and handed them to me. Then she lifted the ladder to her shoulder and we started toward the house. Her face was flushed with cold and exertion. She wore a sweatshirt that was too big for her, the sleeves rolled up over mismatched gloves. Some of the hair she'd tucked under a black watch cap had come loose and stuck out every which way around her face. I thought she looked sexier than hell.

"The house smells good," I said. "You made cookies."

"I did," she replied. "And I plan to make biscuits to go with your stew. Let me get cleaned up and then we can eat. Did you have a good week?"

"Not bad," I replied. "We didn't have many classes. The next group doesn't come in for another month. Instead, the FBI was there with their stuff. Most of us had to attend classes instead of teach them."

"That's a switch," Libby said. "Did you behave?"

She grinned, hooked a finger through my belt loop, and held on to me while we crossed the lawn. She walked so close that I could feel the warmth of her body. In the basement, she put the ladder on its rack and took the clippers from me. She wiped them clean, spayed them with lubricant, and put them in a barrel with other garden tools. She held a hand out for the saw.

"It was interesting this time," I said, watching her work. "They were giving case studies of crimes that got away from them."

"What do you mean?" she asked. "Crimes they haven't been able to solve?"

"They talked about that and crimes they thought they'd solved but it turned out they had the wrong person," I replied as I followed her up the stairs. "And a couple of cases where there were so many legal issues that they decided not to continue investigating. I never thought I'd see the day when the FBI confessed to failure, but this time I think they did."

When we got to the kitchen, Libby repeated my actions at the crock pot and seemed to think the contents were as perfect as I did. As I opened the fridge, she gently rubbed her hand up and down my back.

"Can you wait ten minutes?" she asked. "I would really like a shower. I've been out there for hours. I need to clean up and get warm."

"Sure," I said. "I'll make a salad."

She disappeared down the hall, and I heard her footsteps cross our bedroom. I got out the lettuce and tomatoes and put them on the cutting board. As I took plates from the cupboard, I heard the water come on in the shower. I set the plates on the counter and went down the hall.

In our room, I added my clothes to hers on the bench at the foot of the bed. I tapped on the bathroom door and went in. Libby cracked the shower door and peeked out at me. She grinned when she saw that I'd taken off my clothes.

"May I?" I asked with a bow and a grin

She paused, gave me a mock frown, and nodded. She pushed the shower door open and I stepped in beside her.

She'd been rinsing shampoo from her hair when I interrupted her. It was times like this that I remembered the knitting needle in her hair that first time I saw her standing angry in Lt. Bradshaw's office. Every time I saw her like this, I was amazed. I was amazed at her, amazed at nature, amazed I could feel this way after all my years alone.

The curly, unruly hair she used a knitting needle to hold in place fell past her waist when it was wet. It fell past her waist and was as straight as a string pulled tight between my fingers. In the hours it took to dry, her straight hair shortened into waves and then the waves shortened into the unruly curls I loved. Under the water, I ran my hands over her head and down her back. I pressed the water from her hair as I moved my hand only to have the spray soak it again. It felt so different from the curly stuff I played with when it was dry that I had a hard time keeping my hands off it.

Libby closed her eyes. She pressed against me and laughed. She laughed that throaty laugh that aroused me and gave me so much joy.

An hour later we put on our robes and wandered back to the kitchen. She dished up the stew while I tore lettuce leaves and poured dressing. We ate beef stew and salads sitting thigh-to-thigh under the blank wall where a black and red rooster with beady eyes used to live. She never did make my biscuits.

Libby liked Marta's kitchen. It had two ovens and a large island with plenty of workspace. They sat on stools with mugs of coffee in front of them. They talked while shouts and other kid noise echoed through the house. Bags of flour and sugar sat on the kitchen counter along with the rest of the ingredients needed to make Christmas cookies. A large pot of Marta's homemade tortilla soup bubbled on a back burner.

"I think we may have bitten off more than we can chew this time," Marta laughed.

To start the holidays of right, the women had decided to help the kids make cookies to share with friends and family. Today was the day for that. Susan and Connie had dropped their kids off at Marta's on their was to work. Marta provided the space and Libby provided the ingredients for the baking day.

"They'll be fine," Libby replied. "Last year, BB's had eighteen kids during the holidays. I had help keeping them on task when we made cookies, but you and I should be able to handle a crew this small."

"What are we making?" Marta asked. "I hope it's not gingerbread."

"No gingerbread," Libby laughed. "My two cents' worth is that most people don't like gingerbread no matter what they say. I think they're deceived by the wonderful smell, but the taste doesn't live up to expectations. I've fed a lot of birds with uneaten gingerbread cookies. Gingerbread and fruitcake make very good birdfeed."

"My sentiments exactly," Marta said. "But I think Uncle Glenn likes gingerbread."

"Well, I didn't get what we need to make them, so he'll have to eat something else," Libby said. "The kids will make pecan sandies, sugar cookies, and chocolate with white chips. I've got powdered sugar for frosting and sprinkles in three different colors. If you feel brave, we can color part of the sugar cookie dough and make red and green checkerboards. It's not hard."

"You like this, don't you?" Marta asked. "I mean, you really like kids."

"I do," Libby said. "And kids like me. Even when I was a kid, kids liked me."

"So you and Tanner will have a brood," Marta said with a smile. "Mom and Dad will like that. They know they aren't getting any more from me or Randall."

"We need to get married first," Libby laughed.

"You've been wearing that ring a long time," Marta said. "Just set a date and do it."

"My two cents' worth is that we both feel married," Libby replied. "That's why we can't seem to get on with it. We're already married so there's no reason to get married. Does that make sense?"

"No," Marta said with a grin. "I loved our wedding. One of my favorite memories is the way he looked at me as I walked down the aisle to him. When we fight, I make myself remember that moment and I know we can work anything out."

"Well," Libby said, "if we do get married, it won't be like that. My two cents' worth is that we'll have something very small and quite. We haven't really talked about it. Or kids. We haven't talked about kids, either."

"You will," Marta said as she set down her empty mug. "I guess we should get started on the cookies. Ready?"

At the end of the day, Susan and Connie arrived for their kids. Each child left with a plate piled with cookies and the mothers with a container of Marta's soup.

When they were gone, Libby put the last of the flour and sugar in a bag with her share of the soup. She hugged Marta, picked up the bag and her own plate of cookies, and headed home.

Tanner had called to say he was hungry for ribs and was taking her to Chucky's for dinner. She didn't think he'd mind if she changed his plan. At home she put the cookies on the counter. She poured the soup in a pan to warm and made a vegetable plate. She took a bag of crackers from the cupboard, put a handful in a bowl, and set it on the counter.

Then she took the cookies to their office. She lit the fire and moved the chairs inches closer to the fireplace. When he got home, she'd bring everything in here where they'd be warm and close and could talk. A quiet evening was what she thought Tanner needed after a week at the academy. He could take her for ribs tomorrow.

I stay in a state of wonder about Libby's body. Because of the heavy work I see her doing in the yard, I expect it to be less feminine and more muscular the next time we're together. She may be able to move cement and chop down trees, but her body stays amazingly soft. When I pull her into my arms, I marveled that I can touch such a soft, warm body. I also marvel that it returns the affection to me, touch for touch.

Even better, she is the first woman I've made love to who laughs. It sounds cliché, but her laughter while we're tangled together is like tinkling bells or water rippling over stones. The sound is soft and throaty and makes me laugh in return.

The first night I stayed at her apartment we'd been to a movie and ended up necking like teenagers at the door when I brought her home. We managed to get inside before she tugged my shirttail out and held me away from her to undo the buttons. I closed my eyes, leaned against the door, and tried to relax. When her palms rubbed across my bare chest and her thumbs found my nipples, I groaned. Her laughter started with a swallowed breath and then tinkled over her lips. I opened my eyes and saw her looking at my body. Her arms went around my neck and she kissed me while we made our way down the hall to her bedroom.

I wasn't sure about the laugh, wasn't sure what it meant. But it came again when I undid her bra and pulled her against me. It came again when she tugged my shorts away and I was hard against her. When I was finally inside her and paused before going on, she wrapped her arms and legs around me and laughed a thank you into my ear. I could feel the laughter in her chest before it reached my ear. I couldn't help laughing back.

At first I thought she laughed because she was inexperienced. But she knew what she was doing and what she needed to do to please us both, so that wasn't it. Then I thought she laughed because we were new to each other and neither of us had had a lover in a while. But it flowed over us nearly every time we were together even when the newness had worn off. It still happens when we're together, alone and naked. I wait to hear it. Here we are, two naked people arousing each other, and we laugh. It makes things even more special.

I'd pretty much stopped sleeping my first year as a cop. I'd sleep for a while, get up and roam my apartment, and then go back to bed for a few more hours of sleep. Maryanne, my only live-in girlfriend, complained about that the whole time she lived with me. But I couldn't help myself. I just didn't sleep through the night.

That first night with Libby, I expected to continue my pattern. We snuggled up spoon fashion after we made love and I tucked her head under my chin, brushing her hair down tight to keep it out of my nose. I figured I'd doze off and then wake up long before morning like I always did. I planned to be as quiet as I could when I left the bed since I didn't know if she was a light sleeper.

The next thing I knew, I came slowly awake with something wonderfully warm against my belly. Thinking I was with Maryanne, I reached down to pat her hip to let her know I was getting up. But instead of the narrow bones I expected, I felt a curve so soft it made me open my eyes. Not only was Maryanne not in bed beside me but sunshine was coming in the curtains we'd forgotten to close. I'd slept through the night with my belly against Libby's curvy behind. I hadn't even woken when her hair came loose and I started breathing it in.

I lifted my head to look at Libby. She arched her back in a stretch, turned over, and pressed her breasts against me. My arm went around her.

"Good morning," she said into my neck. "Did you sleep?"

I didn't answer. My mouth found hers and my hands found her curves again. She laughed and reached for me. Later we pulled the covers back over us to sleep for a while before she got up to make coffee.

From then on, I slept through the night as long as Libby was in bed with me. Some nights, she'd move as far away from me as she could get saying *"It's way too hot"*. But as long as she was there, as long as I could reach out and brush my fingertips against her, I could sleep. Sometimes the nights at the academy seem endless without her.

"Libby, Dear."

Libby recognized the warm voice of Mrs. Cochran, one of The Bertram House's wealthiest and most consistent supporters. The woman had paid for the Holiday Inn banquet rooms for BB's last two fundraisers. At each event, she put her own crystal vase on the sign-in table for donations and started them off with several twenty dollar bills.

"Hi, Mrs. Cochran," she replied. "It's good to hear from you."

"It will get even better," Mrs. Cochran said with a laugh. "I want you to go to Sears and get our kids some new shoes."

"That's very generous," Libby said. "But I think they're okay with shoes right now. They get a new pair when school starts. By Christmas, they've usually grown and need new ones. And at Eastertime we check to see who needs them. You might want to save your money for something they need more than shoes."

"Nonsense," Mrs. Cochran said. "Kids always need shoes. And I was thinking about the warm weather and all the things kids like to do outdoors. We wore plain Keds when I was their age, but kids these days needs a lot more than Keds, don't they."

"They sure do," Libby laughed. "Is there something special you want them to get? I mean, are you saying they need to buy cross trainers or running shoes? Do you want the boys to get high tops?"

"What I want is for them to have something new that's theirs and that lets them play outside with the other kids in comfort," Mrs. Cochran replied. "I don't know what a cross trainer is, and I don't need to know."

"Some of their shoes cost seventy dollars," Libby said soberly. "So if you buy a pair of shoes for each of the fifteen kids we have here now, it will be over a thousand dollars. And if we temporarily shelter others from the police that day, it will be even more. We'd have to include them. My two cents' worth is that you'd be spending a lot of money. Are you sure you want to do that?"

"I do," Mrs. Cochran said firmly. "I know you have other needs, but this is what I want to do to start them out for the summer. Did you know that I'm friends with the manager of the Sears store at the mall?"

"No," Libby said. "But I'm not surprised. That explains why you want us to go there."

"No," Mrs. Cochran said, laughter in her voice. "That's not why I want you to buy the shoes there. The reason you're taking the kids to that store is that I get to be the salesclerk."

"What?" Libby asked.

"The salesclerk," Mrs. Cochran laughed. "I get to be the salesclerk in the Sears shoe department when you bring the kids in."

"Why would you do that?" Libby laughed back.

"When I was a girl," Mrs. Cochran said in a confidential tone, "I worked in a women's clothing store until I married Mr. Cochran and became a housewife. I loved that job. I missed that job even after I had babies and had plenty to do in the house. So, I've arranged to be there when you take the kids in for their shoes."

"You're going to talk with them about the pros and cons of footwear?" Libby aksed.

"No," Mrs. Cochran laughed back. "I'm going to be at the register and put the shoes in the bags once you've helped them pick out what they want."

"Mrs. Cochran, you're too much," Libby laughed again. "I guess you want to see where your money is going. You're checking up on us again, huh?"

"Not at all," Mrs. Cochran replied. "I need a little fun in my life, that's all. I need to be around young people to lift my spirits. Don't you think watching those kids pick out shoes and try them on will lift my spirits? I can almost hear their chatter. And don't you think it will be great fun watching the real salespeople try to figure out why their manager is making them to pretend this old, gray-haired lady is one of them?"

"It will," Libby said. "I love going with the kids. They have such a different view of things, don't they?"

"Yes," Mrs. Cochran said. "What do you think would happen if I put something special in each of those bags with the new shoes?"

"Something special like what?" Libby asked.

"Something special like a couple of ten dollar bills," Mrs. Cochran said. "Or maybe a gift card for Dairy Queen or something like that."

"Hmm," Libby said. "Gift cars would be great for the older kids, but it wouldn't matter to the little ones. Maybe cash is the better idea."

"Of course, if we did anything like that, you or someone else from BB's would have to take the kids to Dairy Queen," Mrs. Cochran continued. "I suppose I'd need to give another gift card to the shelter to pay for the volunteers' ice cream. Will you be buying shoes for yourself while you're shopping with the kids? I could slip that the gift card in your bag with your new shoes just like I'm going to for the kids."

Libby laughed. This woman had lost four infants before they turned two. She had grown children who lived out of state and rarely came to visit. And she'd had an adoring husband until he died of colon cancer fifteen years before. After his death, she set up substantial trusts for her children and grandchildren and still had enough money to travel and do whatever she wanted to do. Besides traveling, what she wanted to do was improve her community. Her humor and generosity were a constant Libby and the Bertram House had come to depend on.

"We can work out the details on that," she said. "Let me talk with Sam and see when we can get all the kids to the store. Is there a specific day you'd like to me try for?"

"Don't do it on the 18th," Mrs. Cochran replied. "That's the day I get my hair done."

"Okay," Libby replied.

"I have one other idea to run by you," Mrs. Cochran said. "Would you check on that amusement park in Lamberth and see what it costs to rent it for a day?"

"I'm sure it would be a lot of money," Libby said. "But I'll check. What are you thinking?"

"I'm thinking that if I rented it for the day after school gets out in June, BB's kids and their friends could start the summer off right," Mrs. Cochran said. "I know we'd have to figure out how to get everyone there and have release slips like they do for school field trips, but I'd like to do it. I don't know if we want BB's kids to invite the rest of their schools to come, but it's something we can to think about. It would help their self-esteem, give them something to be proud of, don't you think?"

"I don't know what I think," Libby replied. "My two cents' worth is that you're very generous. I don't know about anything else right now."

"Well, you check on the cost," Mrs. Cochran said. "Then we can talk again and see about taking the suggestion to BB's board for approval."

"I'll get started on it today," Libby replied. "And I'll let you know about the Sears day. Thank you so much."

"Don't thank me," Mrs. Cochran said. "Thank Mr. Cochran. He left me more than I can spend. I have to get creative. We'll talk soon."

Libby wasn't in bed when I woke late Saturday and the clock told me I'd missed the entire morning. I rolled to her side of the bed and buried my face in her pillow. The sheets were cold, but her smell was there. I got up, put on my tatty robe and went to find coffee.

While a fresh pot of coffee dripped behind me, I stood at the kitchen window and watched Libby work. She was upset again. I could tell from the way she wielded the red saw. We'd been living together for nearly three years, and I'd learned to recognize her moods pretty quickly. Working fast and furious in the yard was a sure sign that something was wrong in her world.

That spring, one of the apple trees had failed to send out leaves. Libby tested a few branches, deemed it still alive, and waited for the year to progress to see if it would survive. But it was obvious the tree was dead long before fall rolled around. The leaves never came and the smaller limbs dried out. We were well into fall now. All the trees had dropped their leaves and stood bare against the gray sky. I didn't know she'd decided to cut down the tree at this particular time, but she was working at it with a vengeance.

As I'd seen her do many times, she stood on a ladder, sawing angrily at the lowest branch. When it fell, she went up a step and sawed at the next branch. When four branches were on the ground, she climbed down and picked up the clippers. In brisk, angry movements, she snipped the limbs from the thick branches. She cut the limbs into smaller and smaller pieces before carrying them further from the house to a burn pile that was out of my sight. Using the red saw again, she cut the branches into fireplace-size logs. She climbed the ladder and started the process over again on more branches.

I knew better than to interrupt when she was this upset. By the time she finished what she was doing and loaded the logs into a wheelbarrow, she'd feel better and might even be willing to talk. I put on a pair of jeans and took my coffee outside to settle under a blanket with a National Geographic. Now and then, I'd look up to check on Libby. I refilled my cup often enough that I emptied the pot. Hours later when I was finally hungry and went inside to figure out what to feed us, she was as industrious as ever.

I was putting salads on the table when I saw her pushing the wheelbarrow toward the house. I went out to help empty the logs, and neither of us said anything as we stacked them against the back wall. Then I pushed the wheelbarrow to the apple trees while Libby washed up. She was sitting on the bottom stair taking off her boots when I came into the basement.

"Hungry?" I asked.

"I could eat," she said.

I held out a hand, pulled her to her feet, and turned her up the stairs. She sat in her usual chair, poured dressing on her salad, and picked up her fork. I went to the stove and put soup in two bowls. After setting them on the table, I opened the fridge and got out a bottle of wine. I pulled dinner rolls from the oven where they'd been warming. When I sat across from Libby, she had nearly finished her salad. I poured wine and handed her a glass. She put it to her lips and took a deep sip. She swirled it around in her mouth, swallow, and sighed.

"Thanks," she said. "I was hungrier than I knew."

"Uh, huh," I said. "And angrier. What's up?"

"We got some new kids in on Monday," she said.

"Uh, huh," I said.

This was nothing new. Kids came and went though The Bertram House nearly every day. But I'd have to wait until she was ready or I wouldn't get any details about these new kids. I buttered a roll and started on my soup.

Every now and then when I feel like cooking, I make a big pot of barley soup or chili. We have it for supper a couple of nights in a row, and then I freeze the rest for days when neither of us is up to cooking.

We add bread and salad and maybe some dessert and have a perfectly good meal without much work. This was one of the days I was grateful for the freezer.

Libby's glass was empty. I poured more wine into it and watched her butter a roll. An early evening was settling in around the house. I thought about turning on some light but didn't get up to do it.

"Tanner," she said. "I don't know how much longer I can do this job."

I raised my eyebrows. She loved her job. She loved the kids. The Bertram House was her second home just like the academy was mine.

"How so?" I asked. "You love your job."

"Past tense," she said. "I loved this job."

"What's changed?" I asked.

She broke her roll into pieces and dropped them into her soup. We ate in silence for a few minutes. I make good soup, if I do say so myself. I hoped she'd want a second helping. That would mean she was calming down a little.

"It's all about numbers now," she replied. "My two cents' worth is that we used to have judges who considered the kids and their needs. Maybe they've all retired because I don't see them anymore. Now it's all about how many kids come in and how many kids go out. Nobody asks whether or not where they go is the best thing for them. Get them in, get them out as fast as we can. That seems to be the courts' new creed."

"Well," I said. "From what I can see, there are more people coming into the system. Maybe the system can't handle the increase. Maybe they need new rules."

"Yes," Libby said passionately. "They need new rules for the adults who break the law. But they don't need new rules for the kids who get left behind by those adults. If anything, those kids need more compassion than ever. And it's gone, Tanner. Compassion and caring are completely gone from what we do."

"Who are the new kids?" I asked softly.

"A boy and his twin sisters," Libby replied. She buttered another roll and put a piece in her mouth. "He's four years old. His sisters will be two next month."

"You don't usually know that do you?" I asked. "Don't you usually have to guess their ages based on a doctor's exam?"

"These three were left on the steps of St. Augustine's Sunday night," Libby replied with the hitch in her voice I'd heard many times when she talked about kids. "There was a diaper bag complete with crackers and cheese, a couple of kid-sized blankets, and birth certificates for the three of them. The cleaning company found them when they came to work at eleven o'clock. They found big brother sound asleep leaning against the front door holding one of his sisters' heads on each of his thighs so they had pillows."

I waited while she swallowed hard and blinked back tears.

"He covered them with the blankets," she said. She looked at me with hard eyes. "But they were sitting on cold cement stairs at 11 o'clock at night. Cement, Tanner. You can't tell me those little blankets did any good against cold cement."

Unexpectedly, Libby was crying. I took two steps around the table, stood her up, and put my arms around her. She sobbed into my chest. I held on and let her cry.

"There is something so wrong with us," she said when she stopped shaking. "Humans are terrible people."

I smiled at that. I thought of all the things I'd seen on the job and knew she was right. Libby pulled away from me and smoothed the front of my shirt.

"We put them in a room together at BB's," she continued, and we made sure each of the girls had her own blanket. When the night monitors made their rounds, they found the three of them asleep in one bed, all tumbled up in the sheets and blankets. I'm so glad I didn't see them like that. It would have broken my heart."

It didn't matter that she hadn't seen them tumbled together. Her heart was broken just hearing about it. I put my hands on her cheeks and kissed her forehead. There was nothing I could say that would help.

"I was at their hearing in Family Court this morning," she said. She put her arms around me again and rested her face on my chest.

This wasn't news. She often went to court.

"They aren't assigned to me," she continued, her breath warm on my chest through the fabric of my shirt. "They have a lawyer and a counselor. I wasn't supposed to be there. It was crazy, Tanner. The judgment doesn't make sense. The judge is allowing thirty days for the cops to find the parents or for them to come forward on their own. If they don't, the kids will be separated and sent to different foster homes."

"What?" I asked. Her last words were muffled against me. I wasn't sure what she'd said.

"What a joke," she said. She let go of me and sat back down at the table. "The court is going to run a legal in the papers letting the parents know the kids will be adopted out if they don't come forward in thirty days. What do they think? That people who leave their kids like that read the legal section of the paper?"

"Libby…" I started.

"I know what you're going to say," she interrupted. She couldn't stop talking, which was unusual for her. "You're going to say that there is nothing else to do to find the parents. I guess I can understand that. But I don't know why we can't keep the kids together. My two cents' worth is that we should at least try to put them in one foster home or structure one adoption. I know it's a lot. Do you remember Christopher and Molly?"

"Christopher as in the kid living in a car and stealing to feed his sister?" I asked. She'd caught me off guard with a question in the middle of her anger. "Yes. I remember Christopher."

"It's the same situation," Libby said. "An older brother taking care of a younger sister. The judge who heard Christopher's case told us we needed to find…he said *needed* to find…a foster home that would take both of them. He told Christopher that even though he broke the law doing it, he'd done a good job taking care of Molly. And he said Christopher deserved…he said *deserved*, Tanner…deserved to be placed with his sister. He told us we'd better find a place where that would work."

"Those two were older. Libby," I said. "These three are young. I think they'll be fine if they're separated."

"I know this little boy is only four years old," Libby said. "But he got in that diaper bag to give his sisters something to eat. He got out the blankets to keep them warm, and he knew enough to use his legs for pillows. My two cents' worth is that he deserves to stay with them."

"Libby…" I started to say.

"And the judge," Libby interrupted angrily, her voice rising with every word. "He didn't even meet with them. He talked about them by their case number. I don't think he looked up from his paperwork once during the whole hearing. My two cents' worth is that judges should have to meet these kids before they pass judgment. They should have to look them in the eye and see that what they're doing affects real people."

"Libby," I said when she took a breath. "They're so young. They won't remember any of this in a few years. If they get placed with good parents, they'll do fine."

"How do you know that?" she demanded. "The girls may be too young to remember anything. But the boy will. He'll grow up knowing something happened. He may not know exactly what's wrong, but I think something will be missing from his soul. My two cents' worth is that even after he forgets he had sisters, he'll feel like something is missing. What we do to these kids is so wrong."

"You've done the best you can for a long time," I said softly, trying to calm her down. "But even you can only do so much. You have to depend on the system to do its best."

Libby nodded. She used her napkin to dry her face and blow her nose.

"This might be the straw that breaks me, Tanner," she said. "My heart is breaking for these kids. What kind of parents leave their kids like that? How can they walk away and take no responsibility? I don't understand."

I thought about her mother and all the hurtful questions she'd asked through the years. I thought how Libby had been responsible for her mother the whole time she'd been responsible for the kids at BB's. But I couldn't say anything about that.

What I said was, "You can't understand because you're the opposite of who they are. You've been responsible all your life. Hell, in your job you've taken on other people's responsibilities. Of course you can't understand. But you've done your best, Babe. No one could have done any better than you have."

"There has to be something else I can do," she said. "I don't know what, but there has to be something more I can do for these kids."

Tuesday after class my cell phone rang. I was surprised to have a call at that time of day. Libby called me in the evening after she'd eaten, and I rarely heard from anyone else when I was teaching.

"Hey, little brother," Randy said. "Do you have any vacation time saved up?"

"Some," I replied. "Why?"

"Remember that cabin Uncle Glenn bought in Idaho?" he asked.

"Sure," I said.

"He's thinking about going out there at the end of the month," Randy replied. "Dad's probably going with him and I'm thinking about going along. Why don't you come with us?"

"Who all is going?' I asked. "Are you driving?"

"Dad's thinking about asking Bill to go along, if that's okay with you," he answered. "I'm thinking about taking my kid, so that would be five unless you come with us. We're going to fly into Idaho Falls and rent a car for the rest of the trip. I know Libby's alone a lot already, but if you could come with us, it'd be great."

"Hmm," I said. "I'll think about it. I'll let you know after I talk with Libby."

"Okay," Randy said.

I didn't think about it until I was headed home on Friday.

I had barely gotten my driver's license the first time we went to Idaho. The leaves were changing color as we followed Uncle Glenn across three states. Our two-truck caravan, Dad and Uncle Glenn in the lead with Randy and me following, was filled with tools, curtain rods, used pots, pans and dishes, and a mish-mash of things needed to furnish a cabin. Mom and Aunt Jannette had gone through their kitchens and linen closets for anything Uncle Glenn might need while Dad sorted through the garage to put together a toolkit for him.

Uncle Glenn had found a tiny ad selling a cabin on Beaver Lake north of Idaho Falls in the back of one of his hunting magazines. After a call to the owner, he gave it a lot of thought before deciding to buy the place. My parents tried to talk him out of it, but in the end he said he wanted someplace where he could get away from all of us. He said Idaho seemed like a good place to do that.

Randy and I figured the cabin wouldn't get much use. Uncle Glenn was a homebody. He and Dad seldom when further away than a campground near Lamberth, and they only went there when either Mom or Aunt Jannette convinced them she needed a break. Then they'd dutifully load a truck with camping gear and head off for a few days of fishing. Mom and Aunt Jannette would disappear for at least a day and come home with new hair and painted nails. Marta joined Randy and I making fun of them until the day she was old enough to be invited along. Then she quickly changed her tune.

After a couple of days following Uncle Glenn across arid land, I was happy to see that the cabin really was on a lake. When I saw the large cabin with faded signs and a Dutch door marked BAIT, I knew someone had dreamed of making money on a small compound with a store, a boat dock, and a cluster of rental cabins. Several of the cabins were falling down, but there were four or five like the Uncle Glenn's that were still sturdy with steep roofs and parking under the main floor. I guessed that the roofs and the covered parking spots had to do with the amount of snow that fell each winter.

The screen door slapped Uncle Glenn on the butt as he fitted the key in the lock. He pushed the door open and stepped back to let Dad go in first. Randy and I waited on the porch until Uncle Glenn had followed Dad through the door.

"Wow," Randy said when we were inside. He dropped the box he was carrying and turned in a circle looking up at streams of colored light coming from the loft.

"Wow is right," Dad said. He was looking at the three-seat counter and the old enamel cook stove.

"I like it," Uncle Glenn said. He was rubbing his hand over a black pot-bellied stove and looking at the shoulder high stack of firewood near the door we'd come through.

I didn't say a word. The cabin was not small. It was tiny. Besides the stove and the counter, there was barely space for a couch and a recliner in the downstairs room. A door stood open to a bathroom with a toilet, sink, and shower stall so close together I wasn't sure any of us could turn around in there.

Randy was climbing the ladder to the loft. Dad was standing on the small porch outside the door in the back wall. And Uncle Glenn was still touching the stove. I decided to join Randy.

The colored light was coming from two stained glass windows set in the roof. Pieces of red, yellow and orange glass were leaded together in rose patterns that changed as shadows moved in the wind. The windows were spectacular. I was relieved when I looked closer and saw that the leaded panes were sandwiched in heavier Plexiglas to protect them from the weather.

"Come and see this," Randy called down to Uncle Glenn.

I went down the ladder so there'd be space, and Uncle Glenn and Dad climbed up. I checked the couch and found it folded out into a double bed. At least one person wouldn't be sleeping on the floor in a sleeping bag. Then I went out to the truck and started bringing in the things we'd packed.

After lunch, we walked down to the lake. The front of the cabin had a big green eight on it and we found an eight on the dock. Next to that, an aluminum rowboat, also sporting a green eight, bobbed in the water. Taking turns, we rowed across the lake and back. No one else was around. The place was magical and quiet.

After that, Dad and Uncle Glenn sometimes flew to Idaho and stayed in the cabin for a week. But the place had pretty much disappeared from our memories. I wondered why they were going, and I wondered if I would be comfortable leaving Libby for a week to go along. She was pretty upset about the three kids she'd told me about the week before. I made up my mind to decide after I got home and took a reading on how she was doing. I'd love to see the cabin again, but if Libby was still upset about those kids, I figured Randy and I could go another time.

Libby knocked on Sam Hayes' door. He looked up from the papers on his desk and smiled at her.

"Come on in," he said.

She smiled back and sat across from him.

"I'm going to take the rest of the week off," she said. "There's nothing going on and I have things to catch up on at home. Is that okay with you?"

"Sure," Sam replied with a grin. "Anything I can help with? Anything you can use a couple of the kids for?"

"No," Libby grinned back.

Sam constantly kidded with the kids about renting them out so they could pay for the food they ate. Only the new kids took him seriously. On occasion, both the employees and residents of The Bertram House helped people with a variety of chores, but everything was volunteer. His joking requests for volunteers made BB's a friendly place for everyone. Libby was glad he'd been hired. He was good for the place.

"So we'll see you Monday," Sam said as she went out the door.

Libby stopped at Chucky's on her way home. She got ribs, corn-on-the-cob, and coleslaw, and then debated a slice of the carrot cake displayed next to the cash register. At home, she put everything in the refrigerator.

She was sitting on the floor of their office looking through the bottom drawer with a suitcase next to her when the phone rang.

"Hello," she said.

"Elizabeth. It's your mother," Diana said. "Can you talk? I'm not interrupting anything, am I?"

"I can talk," Libby replied. She thought it was odd that her mother asked if she was interrupting. Diana never did that. The assumption was that if Diana called, the person at the other end had time to talk. "I came home early, so there's nothing to interrupt."

"Oh," Diana said. "Is anything wrong? Are you sick?"

"Nothing's wrong," Libby said in surprise. Her mother asking about her? She never did that. "We didn't have much to do, so I decided to come home early."

"Have you heard from Megan?" Diana asked.

"I never hear from her, Mom," Libby said. She looked at the ceiling, her cheeks puffing out with air. Some things never changed

"Well, when she calls, you tell her hello for me, okay?" Diana said.

"Sure," Libby replied. She'd been tired of this conversation for years, but there was no way around it. She waited, but her mother said nothing more. "Why are you calling Mom?"

"Oh, I did call you, didn't I," Diana laughed. "I was waiting to see why you called, but I guess I called you."

"Yes. You called me," Libby said.

"I wanted to ask you about your Uncle Jarod," Diana said. "Do you remember him?"

"Sure. I remember him," Libby said. She frowned at yet another surprise question. "What do you need to know?"

"Well, did you like him?" Diana asked. "Did you like him and your Uncle Jim? I mean, when you were with your grandmother, did they come around?"

"I like both of them," Libby replied. "Uncle Jarod brought me home after Gram went into the hospital, remember?"

"Did he?" Diana asked. "I don't remember that."

"He and Uncle Jim brought their families to Gram's for Sunday dinner when I lived there," Libby said. "Not every week, but sometimes. I didn't get to know my cousins that well, but they were okay. I got some hand-me-down clothes from the girls. And I remember once when the two of them came and brought trout they'd caught. They wanted Gram to cook it like she did when they were kids. I remember the meat was flaky with a golden, crunchy crust. They told a lot of stories while we ate it."

"But did you like them?" Diana asked. "I mean your uncles. Did you like them?"

"Yes," Libby said cautiously. "I don't really know them. But when they were there, they were nice to me. I still see them once in a while. Yes. I like them both."

"Okay," Diana said abruptly.

"Is something wrong?" Libby asked. "Why are you asking about them?"

"I was just wondering," Diana said. "They were older than me and I don't remember them very well. That's all. I was just wondering if you liked them better than you liked me."

"They're nice, Mom," Libby answered, ignoring the question. "They were good to Gram."

"Okay," Diana said. "Say hello to your sister for me when you hear from her."

"'bye, Mom," Libby said and groaned as she put the phone on the table. She thought her mother asked the strangest questions that weren't connected to anything else. She wondered why, after all these years, her mother was asking her about her uncles.

She worked her way through the files in the bottom drawer, pulling out several and putting them in the suitcase. She skipped the two middle drawers and carefully reviewed the files in the top one. She put one more file in the suitcase.

She set a box of photos on the floor and leaned against the front of the wing chair where she read each night before bed. Methodically going through the pictures, she made a small stack next to her. She went through the box again and selected a couple more to add to the stack. Before she went to the kitchen to eat, she put the photos in the suitcase.

After enjoying her ribs and coleslaw, Libby took a screwdriver from the kitchen drawer and went to the front door. With a dragon head tight in one hand, she undid the screws holding one of the smaller doorknocker to the door. She repeated the process with the other small dragon. She put the screwdriver away, taped the screws to the doorknockers, and put them in the suitcase.

In the basement, she found wood caulk, a sheet of fine sandpaper, a paintbrush, and the can of blue paint she'd used on the front door. She filled the screw holes with caulk and sanded them flat. Then she wiped them clean with her hand. When the caulk was dry, the holes disappeared under the blue paint she carefully applied.

When she took the paint back to the basement, she pulled a plastic tub from under the table and opened it. She took out a canvas bag filled with her grandmother's cake decorating tools. From the shelves, she chose two baby food jars of seeds. Upstairs again, she pushed the bag under the bed she shared with Tanner.

With a cup of tea and the slice of carrot cake beside her, she settled in a wing chair to read. The next morning, Libby finished packing the suitcase with underwear, two pairs of jeans, a pair of Tanner's warm socks, one of his t-shirts, and three of his plaid shirts. She slid the suitcase under the bed and went outside to work in the yard.

Libby was in the yard when I got home. She had cut more two-by-fours to size and was banging them into squares to enlarge the patio. She looked great in jeans and one of my shirts over a t-shirt I wasn't sure was hers or mine. She stopped hammering when she saw me on the walk beside the house with my coat and briefcase in one hand.

"Hey," she called. "You're early."

"Not by much," I said. "Traffic was light for a change."

"We have dinner with your parents tonight," she said as she walked across the yard to me. "I think something's up because Randall's called twice today to see if you're home and to make sure we're coming. He won't tell me anything, but I can tell something is going on."

"Yeah," I said as I gave her a one-armed hug. "They're planning a trip to Idaho. He called me on Tuesday to see if I wanted to go. I'm thinking about it."

"What's in Idaho?" she asked as she followed me into the basement. Always careful with her tools, she'd brought the hammer in with her and set it on the table.

"A cabin," I replied. "A cabin on a lake. Uncle Glenn bought it when Randy was maybe twenty or so. Every now and then he and Dad used to go out there fishing. I don't think anybody's been there in at least a dozen years, but they're planning to go now."

"You should go," Libby said. She wiggled her eyebrows at me. "All that male bonding and stuff."

I raised an eyebrow back at her. She grinned at me and I knew it was okay to go to the cabin.

"Really," she struggled not to smile as she talked with mock seriousness. "My two cents' worth is that the men in your family are not bonded nearly enough. You know. No hugging or back slapping among them. This trip would be a good chance to improve your hugging skills. Would you drive or fly?"

"Fly," I replied. "And rent something in Idaho Falls to drive to the lake."

"You should go," she said again with a big smile.

"You don't even know when they're planning to go," I said as I followed her up the stairs.

"I know it's not this weekend," she said. "Whenever you go, it'll be fine with me."

I grunted. This was not the mood I'd expected her to be in.

"What happened with your kids," I asked. "Tell me all that happened this week."

"The ads were in the paper on Tuesday and they'll run until the end of the month," she said. "The girls slept in their own beds last night. Everybody is happy about that and think they'll be okay by the time we start looking for foster homes."

"What do you think?" I asked.

"My two cents' worth is that the parents should be neutered and then shot," Libby said. "But we know that's not going to happen."

"I mean about the kids," I said. "What do you think about the kids?"

Libby had followed me to the bedroom and watched as I undid my tie and unbuttoned my shirt. She grinned as I pulled my arms through the armholes and leaned to put the shirt in the hamper.

"What kids?" she asked. She was trying hard not to smile.

"Your St. Augustine kids," I said. I stood in front of the dresser and pulled out a drawer.

"They're going to be fine," she said.

She was behind me now and I watched in the mirror as her hands came under my arms and stroked the hair on my chest. She hugged me hard against her. I forgot about the kids.

"We don't have to be at your parents' until six," she said. "Can you think of anything to do until then?"

A week after Tanner's trip to Idaho, daylight was coming through the sheer curtains when Libby opened her eyes. She was on her back with her head resting on Tanner's bent arm. She wondered if he'd have any feeling in it when he woke up. She lay still and let her eyes roam the room.

She loved the wainscoting, the pale green walls, and the wide footstool at the end of the bed. She still liked the bold swatches of color in the old movie posters they'd kept from her old apartment. The tall chest of drawers they'd brought from Tanner's apartment held her favorite framed pictures of the two of them.

She carefully slid one foot from under the covers and down to the floor. Silently, she sat up, pulled the blanket up to cover Tanner's arm, and went to the kitchen. Ignoring the dishes stacked in the sink, she put coffee and water in the coffee maker and found a mix for coffee cake. Ten minutes later she put a pan into the oven and, coffee cup in hand, went to take a shower.

Tanner looked up from his paper when she came back to the kitchen. Her wet hair was pulled into a high mound on the top of her head. He smiled to see the matching letter openers he'd bought as a joke at the Dollar Store sticking through her hair. She kissed the top of his head as she crossed the room to the stove. Without a word, she got out two frying pans and started breakfast.

She worked silently as he read. He set the paper aside when she put a plate in front of him and put the coffee cake in the middle of the table.

"Thanks for doing dinner last night," Libby said as she sat across from him. "I had no energy for it."

"No problem," Tanner replied. "Everybody brought something. And from the number of bottles over there, it looks like we could have served peanut butter sandwiches and no one would have cared."

"My two cents' worth is that we have crazy friends," she said.

"We do," Tanner replied as he cut a piece of coffee cake. "Wonderful, crazy friends. I'm just glad they all get along. I was worried there for a while."

"Why?" Libby asked. "I always thought everyone would get along."

"Well," Tanner said. "You and your gang have college degrees. In fact, Susan's husband has two degrees. Bill and the rest of my friends are blue collar. There's not a college class among them."

"Hmm," Libby said with a smile. "There's not a dummy among them, either."

"True," Tanner replied. "Do you think we'll all go to Mexico next year? It will be a big crowd if we all decide to go."

"My two cents' worth is that the plan will evolve before then," Libby replied. "Another location, maybe, or two shorter vacations together. Maybe we can all go to Idaho and rent cabins by Uncle Glenn's. No matter what we do, I hope it works out. I like the idea of all of us spending time together. We gals can wander off while you guys watch sports. Some of us can sunbathe while everybody else goes hiking. It won't matter were we go."

Maude and Bill had joined Tanner, Libby, Connie and Susan and their husbands for a potluck the night before. For the past year or so, the couples had met at restaurants, took the kids for picnics that ended up as tag football games, and potlucks at one another's homes. This get-together had been last minute, with Bill calling Tanner to see what had happened on the trip to Idaho. Leaving the wives out of it, the men found babysitters, planned the meal, bought groceries, and cooked.

The sink was filled with dirty dishes and the counter cluttered with wine and liquor bottles. Tanner cleared the table and refilled the coffee pot. Libby put plastic wrap over the coffee cake and put it in the refrigerator.

"Do you need to me to do anything before I leave?" Tanner asked.

"No," Libby replied with a laugh. "I'm cleaning this up and going back to bed."

She stood in front of him and placed his hands on her hips. She leaned her head on his chest. Tanner tilted his head to miss the letter openers.

"What are you teaching this week?" she asked.

"Same old, same old," Tanner replied. "If I remember right, this is a small group of newbies and we're trying a different format again. We keep trying to get more information into the same amount of time. But I should be teaching the same thing I always teach. Are you sure you don't want help with this. It looks like we had a lot of fun last night."

"Nah," Libby said. She moved away from him and looked around the room. "I like restoring order. Besides, if you don't help, I get to complain about you."

Tanner grinned and went to pack. Libby filled the sink with hot, soapy water and started cleaning up. Tanner gave her a goodbye hug and kiss, and she watched from the window as he drove away.

She finished the dishes then used the wet rag to wipe down the tables in the living room. She swept the kitchen floor, put the dry dishes away, and took out the garbage. She ran the vacuum cleaner, emptied the bag, and returned the vacuum to the basement.

In their bedroom, she changed the bed sheets and arranged the pillows so Tanner's two round pillows were right where he would sit and read. Then she pulled the suitcase and canvas bag from under the bed. She unzipped the pocket on the side of the suitcase and put her fingers inside. She read the back of the postcards before she leaned them against the picture frames on the chest of drawers. Then she placed two shiny copper pennies next to the postcards.

"Be as smart as I think you are, Tanner," she said to the empty room. "Be smart enough to find us."

Part 3

After Libby and the kids disappeared, I found myself under surveillance. When I was teaching, it became routine for a new face to wander into my classroom, take a seat to watch me for a while, and leave before I finished teaching the class.

When I was home, I saw black-and-whites and unmarked cruisers come by at least twice a day. One Saturday, I was sure I saw Farley's personal car drive slowly by. I wondered if my fellow officers came by during the week when I was gone. And I wondered if they came by after I'd gone to bed. It was annoying at first, but it didn't matter. I didn't know where Libby was. I was sure she wasn't coming back. They could watch all they wanted, but they'd never see us together. They could hound me all they wanted and I still couldn't help them find her.

She'd been gone more than a month when I came home from the academy with the constant headache I'd had since she left raging between my ears. I'd taken Advil before I started my drive. Now I needed more.

I'd barely closed the door and dropped my bag on the floor when the kitchen phone started to ring. I debated whether or not to answer it while I scanned the mail. I dropped the envelopes on the table as I snagged the receiver. Anything to make it stop ringing.

"Hello," I said, annoyed.

"This is Allen Ross," an unfamiliar man's voice said. "Am I talking to Tanner Moran?"

"Yes," I replied, my heart now pounding as hard as my head. Allen Ross. Allen Ross. I should know the name, but I couldn't place it.

"I'm calling to talk with you about Elizabeth," he said in a clipped tone I didn't like.

Elizabeth, Elizabeth I thought. It took me a minute to remember that Libby's name was Elizabeth. That minute of silence seemed to upset him.

"I'm married to Diana Lindt. Elizabeth's mother," he continued angrily. "Is this a good time to ask you some questions?"

Libby's mother? Libby's mother's current husband was calling to talk to me? I couldn't get my head around it.

"Uh, yeah," I stammered awkwardly. "But could you hold on a minute. I can call you back if that's better."

"I'll wait," he said.

I got the Advil from the cupboard and swallowed three tablets with a big gulp of water. Then I took a deep breath and calmed myself to talk with this man I'd never met.

"Okay," I said into the receiver. "What was it you wanted?"

"Diana got a letter today," he replied in a cold voice. "She got a letter from Elizabeth."

I was surprised. I hadn't expected anything like this.

"Look at the postmark," I almost yelled at him. "Where was it mailed?"

There was a pause then he said with a calm that infuriated me, "Well, from there. It was mailed from Kingsford Grove."

"What does the letter say?" I asked. I didn't dare hope it would be important.

"It's short," Allen replied. "I'm not going to read it to you, but it basically says that Elizabeth is going away. It says that her cell phone won't work and that Diana shouldn't count on talking with her anymore. Is that true?"

"Yes," I said. I was disappointed. Any hope I had about her letter was gone. "It looks like Libby...Libby took off with some kids from The Bertram House about a month ago."

"The Bertram House?" he asked. "What's that?"

I shook my head impatiently. Libby had talked with her mother often enough that I felt both she and her husband shouldn't need me to tell them about Libby's life. My head was about to fall off my shoulders. And I was fighting tears. Add to that my opinion of a woman who would lie to her daughter for twenty years, and I didn't have a good taste in my mouth. To heck with this man and his questions.

"The Bertram House is where she worked," I said abruptly. I talked fast. Now I was angry and just wanted off the phone. "She took the kids and left without telling anyone where she was going. The police are looking for her, of course, so I'm sure she tossed her cell phone. You should call them since you got a letter from her. They'll be around anyway to talk with you about Libby and where she might have gone."

"Diana doesn't know anything about that," Allen replied. His anger seemed to match mine. "And we certainly have no idea where she might be."

"Me either," I said. "Listen, I don't feel very well. Unless you have something specific to ask, I'm going to hang up. I need to lie down."

"Can Diana call you if she needs to?" he asked before I could hang up. "She used to call Elizabeth when she needed someone to talk to. She'd be so pleased if. . .

"No," I cut him off. "Tell her not to call me. I have nothing to say to her. I'll never have anything to say to her."

I wasn't sure whether Mom asked him to keep an eye on me or not, but Randall showed up on my front porch nearly every Friday for a few months. He brought food and beer and sometimes a movie.

The first week, the only words he spoke were "This is a great couch". I already knew it was a great couch and I wasn't happy that he was there, so I just grunted back and sulked that he was imposing on me. The second week he brought a movie with popcorn and beer. We managed the whole evening without a word to each other. But after that, I looked forward to having him there my when I got back from the academy. He seemed more comfortable, too, so I wasn't surprised when he started in on the questions.

"Remember Ramona from high school?" he asked one night when we took our dirty plates to the kitchen.

"Sure," I replied. "I dated her for, what six, eight months?"

"Remember when she broke up with you?" he asked. "You always said you knew it was coming. Remember? You said she gave off a vibe you knew meant she was interested in someone else. Remember telling me that?"

I nodded. I'd forgotten about it, but he was right. For the last few weeks Ramona and I were together, I expected her to say goodbye to me every time I saw her. And I knew where the conversation was going before he said another word.

"Did you get the vibe from Libby?" he asked.

I shook my head.

"So you're saying you didn't get a vibe from Libby?" he asked, shaking his head in disbelief. "You had no idea this was coming?"

"No vibe," I replied. "We were getting married, Randy. She was happy. I was really happy. She loved working at The Bertram House. She loved those kids and doing whatever she could do for them. Look at this place. She did this. I haven't been around enough to make any difference. Do you think she'd put all this effort into the house if she was planning to leave?"

We jumped at a thump on the kitchen door. A second thump sounded as I reached for the door handle. I shrugged at Randall when I opened the door and no one was there. I closed the door. The thump came again before I got my hand off the knob. I opened the door and stepped out to look around.

"Well, hello," Randall said.

I turned around to see Big Boy at Randall's feet.

"Geez," I said. I crouched down. The big cat crossed the kitchen floor and butted my hand. "Where did you come from, fella?"

"You know him?" Randall asked. "He's huge."

"Yeah," I replied. "This is Big Boy. He used to show up at Libby's apartment. She lived on the second floor and he'd somehow show up on her deck. She kept grilled chicken in the freezer so she'd have something to feed him."

"He was Libby's?" Randall asked. "And she just left him behind when she moved in here with you?"

"It wasn't like that," I answered. "It's more like Libby was his. He wasn't her pet. She never knew when he'd show up. Sometimes he'd be there every night for a week. Sometimes she wouldn't see him for a month or six weeks. When he was there, he'd sit in the kitchen doorway like a Sphinx and watch us. She said he slept at the foot of her bed when I wasn't there. We always wondered if he missed her when she moved over here. We wondered if he'd find her."

Big Boy sat under the table patiently waiting while I found a can of tuna.

"Animals are amazing," Randall said with a shrug. He leaned against the counter and crossed his arms over his chest watching the cat. "Just tell me one thing, Tanner. Are you going to try to find her?"

"I don't know what I'm going to do," I replied. "I can't believe she did this. I can't believe she would put me in this situation. I mean, I'm a cop. This is bad for me. It makes me look like a fool."

"You're not a fool," Randy said. "None of us suspected anything. Even Uncle Glenn says he would never have guessed this ending."

"Well, I feel like a fool," I said. "But at the same time, I know she thinks she did the best thing for those kids."

"Maybe she did," Randy said. "I can't imagine my kids being separated and farmed out to different home to never see each other again. That would be awful for them."

He watched me dump tuna in a bowl and set it on the floor. I filled a second bowl with water and put it under the table. Then I leaned against the counter next to him and we silently watched Big Boy eat. Cool air coming in the open door carried the smell of someone's freshly cut grass.

"I don't know what I'm going to do," I finally said. Big Boy finished eating and cleaned his whiskers before moving to the water dish. "I'm mad and sad and confused. It'll be a while before I figure things out. Besides, I have no idea where to look."

"Well," he said, straightening up and putting his arms around me in a strong, comforting, big-brother hug. "Be sure you talk with me and Dad and Uncle Glenn before you do anything. You'll probably need us to keep you out of trouble."

I nodded and walked him as far as the porch. I watched him walk to his car and drive away. As I closed the door, Big Boy meowed from the floor. I picked up his heavy, furry body intending to go to the kitchen and put him outside. Instead I held him where I could look him in the eye. He blinked and meowed at me. I put him next to my chest and he licked my hands while I cried.

I was in the basement when Connie showed up. I had all of Libby's boxes pulled out from under the table and I'd started going through them. I'd told Connie to come around to the back, so I wasn't surprised when she tapped on the door and walked in. I gave her a quick peck on the cheek and went back to the box I had open.

"What's all this?" she asked, gesturing at the boxes.

"This is the stuff she brought with her from her apartment," I replied and couldn't find them. She hadn't decorated a cake in a while, so I thought maybe they were in one of these boxes."

"Not likely," Connie said.

We stared at each other for a minute.

"Where do you want me to look," she finally said, breaking eye contact.

"I just started," I said. "You take those two, I'll look in these. She kept them in a white bag. A canvas bag about two feet square with a black fabric handle."

We didn't talk while we went through Libby's boxes. In the end, the bag of her grandmother's cake decorating tools wasn't there. We put everything and slid the boxes back under the table. Then we sat on the stairs, and I studied the cracks in the concrete floor.

"You look like hell Tanner," Connie said softly. "How are you doing?"

"I clean up pretty good when I want to," I said. "I can almost pass for the living when I'm at the academy."

"But how are you?" she insisted.

"Honestly?" I asked. She nodded. "I'm broken. My heart is broken and I'm surprised it keeps on beating. My head is broken so bad it hurts all the time. I take so much Advil all of us should buy stock in the company. My spirit is broken and I don't think it's going to heal. I just want to lie down and go to sleep and never get up."

Connie's hands made gentle circles on my back. She rested her head on my shoulder.

"This probably won't help," she said. I could tell she was holding back tears. "But she didn't do this to just you. She did it to all of us. We've been The Three Musketeers since Mr. Polo Shirt dubbed us that in junior high school. My kids keep asking when they get to come over here. Maude's boys keep asking if she's mad at Aunt Libby. A lot of us are hurting, Tanner."

I nodded but couldn't say anything without crying.

"All I can think is that she didn't see any other way to help those kids," she continued. "I hate it. I probably hate it more than you do because I knew her when Megan disappeared. It's like what her father did all over again. The difference is that I know she understands the hurt she left behind. I don't think I'll ever understand why she decided to put us through what she suffered when she was a kid, but I'm sure she thought it was for the best."

"I know," I whispered. "It doesn't help."

We sat side by side and I rested my chin on the top of her head while she rubbed my back. I refused to cry, but tears ran down my face into her hair.

"Allen called me," I said.

"Who?" she asked.

"Allen somebody," I replied. "Crosby? Cross? Something like that. Her mother's husband."

Connie sat up and looked at me. She reached out and wiped my tears away.

"Al called you," she said, her voice filled with surprise. "Why?"

"Libby sent a letter," I explained. "She sent her mother a letter saying she was going away and that her cell phone wouldn't work and that they probably wouldn't see each other again. He called to see if it was true. He sounded pretty angry that Libby would cut her mother off."

"That's weird," Connie said.

"Yeah, that's what I thought," I said. "What's even weirder is that it was mailed from Kingsford Grove and they got it a month after she left."

"I can explain that," Connie said slowly after giving it some thought. She leaned against me again and put her hand on my back. "At BB's she organizes the mailings. You know, the letters and flyers that go out asking for money. She gets them ready whenever volunteers are available. Sometimes they're ready to go weeks before someone takes them to the Post Office. Boxes of them sit in her office with dates on the end saying when they're supposed to be mailed. All she had to do was put her letter in one of those boxes and it would have been mailed with the rest of them. Nobody would have noticed."

"Hmm," I said. "But why would she send a letter to her mother? She hasn't seen her in all the time we've been together. I know they talk on the phone. Not that often, I think, but they do talk on the phone. Why wouldn't she send me a letter?"

We were quiet a minute while she thought about it. I'd already thought about it and hadn't come up with an answer.

"Because people are watching you," Connie said thoughtfully. "They are, aren't they? The cops are still watching you?"

"Yeah," I sighed. "I suppose they could go through my mail. I'm gone all week and wouldn't notice if something was missing."

"Besides, she knows her mother…who her mother…I don't know how to say this," Connie said. "Megan disappeared. You know that. Libby finally accepted that her sister was dead. But Diana never did. She's always been weird about Megan."

I wanted to tell her what Uncle Glenn had learned. I thought it was only fair that one of Libby's best friends knew that Diana had been deliberately cruel to her daughter all those years. Maybe she would, in turn, be cruel to Diana. I thought that was fair. But I hadn't told Libby what I knew. Since I hadn't, I didn't tell Connie either.

"You never met Diana, did you?" Connie asked.

I shook my head.

"Every time she talks to Libby, she asks if Meg has called," Connie continued. "That started in college and was still going on as far as I know. I think maybe Libby is trying to take care of Diana again. She couldn't have her mother calling and calling and not getting an answer. Diana would go over the edge if that happened. So Libby tried to let her know what was going on without really telling her what was going on."

We sat leaning against each other for a long time without talking. I was comforted by her warm cheek resting against my arm. Finally Connie stood up.

"She loves you, Tanner," she said. "It probably doesn't seem like she does, but I've never seen her the way she is with you. She didn't really do this to you. She didn't do this to Diana or Susan or me or anyone else. She did it *for* those kids. I have to believe she's safe someplace and those kids are together and safe with her. She knew we could take care of ourselves. Those kids couldn't so she did it for them."

"Yeah, I know" I said. "It doesn't help."

I stood up and we walked arm-in-arm around the house to her car.

I wanted to close at least one door of my life with Libby. So when Sam Hayes called asking me to come by, I stopped at The Bertram House one Friday afternoon on my way home from the academy. I'd been there a few times with Libby but I'd forgotten how big it was. I sat in the car looking at the old house and tried to figure out how many times Libby had walked through the front door. I gave up and went inside.

Sam stood when I came into his office. Libby had told me the room was warm and comfortable. I couldn't really tell because there boxes on the floor and the shelves were half empty. We shook hands and introduced ourselves.

"Sorry this took so long," he explained as I sat in a chair in front of his desk. "After the police were here, we found a few of Libby's things in some of the other rooms. You know, a mug in the break room, one of her coats on a rack."

I nodded. He pushed a small box across the desk to me.

"I called the detective to let him know we'd found some things," he continued. "He never called back, and I quite honestly forgot about it."

I nodded again. I knew how things happened when you were busy.

"Anyway," Sam continued. "I'm moving my office to the end of the hall so we can use this room for the library. One of Libby's donors just left us an endowment earmarked for education."

"Good," I said half-heartedly. "She'd be happy about that."

"Yes, she would," Sam replied with a smile. "Anyway, I found the box when I started clearing out the room. I called the cops again and this time they said they didn't need it. I guess they have everything they need from when they did their search."

"Probably," I said. "Their searches are pretty thorough."

"Would you like a tour?" Sam asked, standing up. "I don't think you've ever seen her home away from home, have you?"

"I haven't," I replied. I stood up, too, and picked up the box. "Thanks. But I'd rather not."

He nodded in understanding. We walked out the office door and started down the hall.

"Did she say anything to you?' Sam asked. "I'm guessing she didn't, but I've wondered about it."

"Not a word," I replied. "She talked about this place a lot. She was always talking about the kids and their court cases and how you needed to constantly raise more money. But no. I didn't know she was going to do this."

"I keep thinking I missed some clues," Sam said as we walked. "She was so upset when those kids came in that I decided she couldn't function very well as their advocate. I think that was the only time she ever got angry with me. We've had a lot of differences through the years, but she'd never got mad at me. That time she did. She was so angry I told her to take some time off, which she refused to do. I keep thinking I missed something. I keep thinking I should have known something like this was going to happen."

"Me, too," I replied. "On the other hand, she was good at what she did. She obviously had a plan. It was what, a month between when the judge gave his order and when she left. Nobody can find her, so she had to have a plan to cover her moves. Maybe we didn't miss any clues because she didn't leave any."

"Maybe," Sam said. We stopped at the front door. "I miss her. She held this place together more than anyone else, including me. It's my job and I like being here. But Libby loved it. She loved the kids. She made us laugh and kept us on our toes. She was my friend, Tanner. I'm going to miss her."

"Thanks," I said as we shook hands. "I'll let you know if I hear from her."

He held the door for me and I carried the box to my car. I rolled down the car windows and sat looking at BB's until I thought I could drive. But instead of starting the engine, I opened the box Sam had given me.

Libby smiled up at me. On top of everything else was a silver frame holding Libby and me, cheek-to-cheek, clowning for Maude. I remembered the day in the park with their boys. I remembered all the good food and good times we shared with our friends. A weight started crushing my chest. I closed the box, set it on the passenger seat, and stared at the old house again.

When I was calmer, I headed for home. As I drove, I remembered the day I'd found Waterford and Farley at my front door.

I'd handled them with a bravado I hadn't felt. When Waterford explained the problem, I knew Libby had done something. I didn't let on, but I knew.

Once they were parked at the curb, the three of us waited for the warrant to arrive. I was on my second beer when Dad and Uncle Glenn pulled up. Dad took my beer away and went inside. Uncle Glenn sat down next to me on the step.

"You know this is important, don't you?" he asked, looking at the cruiser at the curb.

I nodded.

"Well," he asked abruptly.

"Hey," I said angrily. "I'm not a kid anymore. I know what is going to happen."

"Good," he replied. "So you know why I want you to go home with your Dad and let me stay here instead."

"It's Farley," I said in a flat voice. "I'm not going anywhere."

"That's right," he said. "It's Farley. And that's the best reason for you to leave as soon as you're served."

Behind us, Dad came out the door and stood watching the black-and-whites lining up behind the cruiser.

"I don't want him in my house," I said, my voice rising. The weight was heavy on my chest again. My hands were shaking. I'd never felt so enraged.

"No choice, Tanner," he said. "I'll stay and keep an eye on him."

"I don't trust him," I said. "I don't want him in my house."

"You don't have a choice," he said.

Dad came down the stairs and stood in front of us.

"Stand up," Uncle Glenn ordered. I didn't move.

Waterford and Farley got out of the cruise. A uniformed officer handed Farley an envelope. I stood up when he grinned in my direction.

"I called the chief," Uncle Glenn said. He maneuvered me so I was standing between him and Dad. I felt like a kid between them, but I didn't feel safe like I had back then.

"He's sending Lt. Bradford to oversee this," Uncle Glenn continued.

The cops waited as Farley scanned the warrant. He handed it to Waterford, who also looked it over as another cruiser pulled up. Lt. Bradford got out and held his hand out for the warrant.

"You made a deal for me?" I asked, still angry. "I didn't ask you to do that."

We stood in a row watching Lt. Bradshaw point at people as he gave instructions.

"I'm not that powerful," Uncle Glenn grunted as we watched the street empty into my yard. "Just be glad somebody read all those reports you turned in."

Lt. Bradshaw tipped his head at me as he handed me the warrant. I handed it to Uncle Glenn without reading it. As the cops started up the stairs to my house, Dad walked me to his truck and took me to the house where I'd felt safe all my life. I didn't go back to my own house until the next weekend when I finished teaching.

Now, after getting home from my meeting with Sam at BB's, I sat in the car wondering how I was going to forget that day. It still played in my head like a bad movie every time I let my guard down.

I picked up the box of Libby's things and went inside. I set it on the kitchen table, opened it, and took out the silver frame. I rummaged through the rest of the stuff, finding a cloth make-up kit, the coffee mug and jacket Sam talked about, a couple packages of dry noodles, and extra socks and pantyhose. Except for the photo, I didn't want any of it. But neither did anyone at BB's. I closed it up, took it to the basement, and pushed it under the table by the window with the other boxes.

I needed to pack Libby's things and get them out of the house. It was going to be hard for me to stay. I could hire someone to take care of the yard and clean while I was gone during the week. If Libby's things didn't surround me, maybe I'd be okay. If I got rid of her stuff, maybe I really could close the door on that part of my life and move on.

I'd start first thing in the morning with a trip to the grocery store to get boxes.

A year and a half later, I hadn't gotten rid of anything. The house was still too big and too full of memories. I still slept on the couch and cleaned up in the basement shower when I was there. I rarely felt like cooking, so I'd long ago used up the meals we'd frozen and started living on deli food. I knew the rooms we'd shared were gathering dust and I'd eventually need to deal with the things Libby and I had accumulated together. But as long as I was spending most of my time at the academy, I chose to leave things the way they were.

Then one Friday when I got back from teaching, Dad's truck was parked in my driveway. I sighed. I wasn't ready for whatever he wanted. I saw my parents regularly, but it was always at their house. They hadn't been here since Libby left even though they'd had a key since I bought the place. The only time I knew they'd used it was when we went to Mexico and Mom came by to bring in the mail and water the yard.

I unlocked the front door and called out as I went inside. No one answered. I put my briefcase on the sofa and made my way down the stairs and out the door of Libby's storeroom. I found Dad and Uncle Glenn sitting on deck chairs in the backyard, beers in hand, looking at the apple trees. I was surprised to see Big Boy sitting on Uncle Glenn's lap gazing up at his round face and wire-framed glasses through nearly closed eyes. One of Uncle Glenn's big hands ran through the thick, soft fur, making the cat purr deep in his chest.

Uncle Glenn still lived in the apartment above my parents' garage. They'd bought the house after Randall and I left home. Then Marta started college and they built the apartment as a way for her to live at home but feel like she was on her own. Since she left, they rented it to college students for a little more income. No one ever said anything about it, but I was sure Uncle Glenn had the same arrangement. Maybe he got more family dinners than the college kids ever did, but I was sure he paid rent just like any other tenant.

I followed their line of sight and found an industrious redheaded woodpecker in the trees. Libby had picked the apples every fall. She made them into pies, which she froze unbaked and we enjoyed all winter. She made apple butter and applesauce and gave them as gifts during the holidays. Maude took some of the fruit to make her sorbet. Now only one of the trees bore fruit. The others that were still standing were gray skeletons with dead arms reaching to the sky.

"Hey," I said. I took a beer from the cooler between their chairs. "What are you two doing here?"

"That tree's dead, you know," Uncle Glenn said.

"Yeah," I replied. "They're all dead except the one on the end."

"You got any of that apple butter left?' Dad asked. "Libby made some good apple butter. Good pies, too."

"Maybe," I replied. "I haven't looked in a while."

I took a seat in the last lawn chair and we watched the woodpecker for a while.

"They only attack diseased or dead trees, you know," Uncle Glenn said. "I think you've got a smorgasbord for them out there."

"I think that cat was stalking the woodpecker," Dad said. "He wandered over from the trees a while ago. I take it he's the one Randy told us about? Libby's cat?"

"Yeah," I replied. "I guess you could call him Libby's cat."

We sat some more and watched the woodpecker. I drank my beer. Finally, I couldn't stand the silence.

"What are you two doing here?" I asked. "You haven't been here since before Libby left. What's going on?"

Uncle Glenn sat forward to shoo Big Boy off his lap, leaned his elbows on his knees in his familiar pose, and pushed his glasses up on his nose. He looked at me through the wire frames.

"You've been pouting around here long enough, Tanner," he said. "Your Dad and I figured we'd help you clean things out so you can make a new start."

"A new start on what?" I asked angrily. "I don't want a new start."

"Well, call it a new phase, then," Dad said. "Libby's gone. You don't need this big place. You hardly live here. We're going to help you move on."

"In case you two haven't noticed, I haven't been a kid for a long time." I said in a huff. "Since when do you get to make decisions for me?"

Big Boy jumped onto my lap and tucked his nose into my armpit. Then he butted his head against my chest, and I ran a hand down his back. I tugged the stump of his tail and he arched his back asking for more.

"Since you seem to have stopped making them for yourself," Dad said.

"Since you seem to be stuck in the past," Uncle Glenn said at the same time.

I shook my head. I stroked a purring Big Boy and watched the woodpecker drill holes in Libby's tree. It made me want to cry. The weight landed hard on my chest again and I could hardly breathe.

"She's not coming back, Tanner," Uncle Glenn said, his voice a little more gentle than it had been. "If she was, she'd already be here."

"Yeah, well," I said, my watering eyes still on the bright bird. Big Boy's rough tongue licked across my knuckles.

"You should put this place on the market," Dad said. "It's a good time to sell. You'd get enough to live on for a while if you sold right now."

"How much longer do you have at the academy?" Uncle Glenn asked. "You're about ready to retire, aren't you?"

I sighed. They were asking all the questions I'd been asking myself lately. I held up my hands in resignation. They leaned back in their chairs and waited.

"Okay, okay," I said. "I've been thinking about all of this. For your information, I'll have twenty-seven years in next spring. I can retire any time now. The paperwork gets submitted ninety days before I want to leave. That's if I decide to leave. And you're right. I don't need this place. I can sell it and move back into an apartment. There. I said it. Are you two happy now?"

"It isn't us we're worried about," Uncle Glenn said. "You've been stewing too long, Tanner. We're all worried about you."

"You should hear your sister," Dad chuckled. "I never thought I'd see the day she wailed about your condition. I think that girl loves you more that she can admit."

We sat in silence for a while, drinking our beer and thinking our own thoughts. Big Boy circled my lap twice and curled up in a ball with his head tucked in near his belly.

"Doesn't Randall have a friend who sells real estate?" I asked, hating it that I was the one breaking the silence again.

"Gerald Morrison," Dad replied with a nod. "He retired, but his agency's still running. It's called something like City Line Realty. You could talk to them. Or you could call Gerald directly. Randy'll have his number."

"And we'll help you get this place cleaned up and ready to sell," Uncle Glenn said. "Your Mom and Randall and Marta and their kids will help if you ask. Bill and Maude will probably be happy to pitch in. When do you want to get started?"

"You are one pushy guy," I said. "Do you know that?"

"Only when I need to be," he laughed as he stood up.

"If we don't hear from you in a couple of weeks, we'll be back," Dad said.

Big Boy jumped down and circled Dad's legs, waiting to see what they'd do next. I took their beer cans and tossed them into the fire pit with mine. We walked up Libby's concrete path to the front of the house where they each gave me a hug before getting into Dad's truck.

"By the way," Uncle Glenn said as he let me go. "I think you should take that last dragon with you when you move out. That poor thing looks kind of lonesome without his friends."

"What dragon?" I asked.

"Your door knocker," he replied as he pointed at the house. "There used to be three of them on your front door. Now there's only one and he looks pretty sad."

I waved as they went around the driveway and disappeared down the street. Then I climbed the porch stairs with Big Boy at my heels and looked at the door. Under the middle window, the largest dragon was still sticking his forked tongue out at visitors. But his buddies were gone. Their absence made me shiver.

For the first time in a year and a half, I went down the hallway to the bedroom I'd shared with Libby. The bed was still perfectly made with the chocolate and green comforter and round pillows we'd picked when I bought the place. I could see the brown striped towels and shower curtain through the bathroom door. Big Boy jumped onto the bed and sent dust flying. He jumped back down and stood at my feet with his head tilted up at me.

The closet was open. A few empty hangers and Libby's dusty clothes gave testimony to the room's disuse. Dust covered everything. I picked a book up from Libby's bedside table then carefully put it back in the rectangle it had left behind.

I walked across the room and looked out the window into the back yard where I'd watched Libby work so many times. The woodpecker was gone. I could see a pattern of holes on the tree trunk where he'd been working. I turned and scanned the room.

I remembered the day Waterford, Farley, and I waited for the search warrant. I'd been lucky that Lt. Bradshaw was in charge and most of the men who searched my home were friends. If Farley had been alone, the whole house would have been a mess. As it was, they'd been respectful. I had no doubt they'd been as thorough as they would have been with anyone else, but as far as I had been able to tell, nothing was broken or misplaced.

I looked around our room and saw something I didn't remember. Postcards were propped against the picture frames on the chest of drawers. I walked across the room and picked them up. Two dusty pennies sat on the dresser next to the thin lines left behind when I picked up the postcards. I wiped the dust on my pant leg to see the pictures. They were the postcards Bill, Maude, and I had brought to Libby from our trip to Chihuahua. Libby had been sick. She stayed behind when we drove over the mountains to see where Bill's grandfather had homesteaded. She said to bring her postcards and we did.

I'd forgotten about that vacation. I turned the cards over to read the captions. I found Libby's handwriting in the address section of each card, one word on each card. The first read *My,* the second *Two,* and the third *Cents. My Two Cents.* I looked at the pennies on the dresser, blew away the dust that covered them, and looked back at the postcards.

I turned them over one by one and looked at the pictures. Each was a scene from the area around Chihuahua. I'd bought the one showing the broad, flat houses of the Pacquine Ruins since that's where Libby had wanted to go. Maude chose a bright market stall filled with flowers.

Bill opted for a string of sad burrows tied together with mud-caked rope. I turned them over again. *My Two Cents.* Libby hadn't gone with us. She wouldn't remember any of this. Her handwriting should not be on these cards. When had she done this? Why had she done it?

I put the two pennies in my pocket. I looked around the room one more time. Then I went to the living room and plopped on the sofa. Before I was settled, Big Boy jumped onto my lap and curled into a ball. I lined the post cards up in order across my legs where I could read them over his back.

My Two Cents. My Two Cents.

Libby said this all the time. She'd listen to me rant and rave, and then she'd reply with her opinion, her two cents' worth, on my concern. We'd talk about the things we could do, complete with options, and she'd give me her two cents' worth on the plans we'd made.

My Two Cents.

"What do you think, Big Boy?" I asked as I rubbed his soft fur and listened to his rumbling purr. "What's she trying to tell me?"

I fell asleep as the sun went down and the room slowly darkened. I woke up with Big Boy gone, the cards in my lap, and the sun coming through the windows. And I knew. I knew what her two cents' worth was.

Susan spread a blanket over her daughter. Small forms were everywhere in the girl's room. Her son and daughter, Marta's three kids, and Maude's three boys were napping after playing together all morning. Their lunch had been a noisy affair and it had taken her reading three books for them to calm down enough to sleep. She knew they'd sleep hard and probably need to be woken up. Her kids were always grumpy when she had to do that. She thought it would be a long afternoon with eight disgruntled kids.

While she watched the kids, her friends had headed to Tanner's to see how much packing needed to be done and decide the best way to do it. From there, they were going to the hardware store for bags and tape, followed by a stop at the liquor store for boxes. She'd heard them sneak into the house while she read to the kids.

Connie handed her a glass of iced tea when she entered the living room. Susan took a seat on the floor in front of the chair Marta occupied. Maude sat on the couch with her legs across the cushion.

"Tanner says he wants to get rid of everything," Marta began.

"What's he going to do?" Connie asked.

"It's crazy," Marta replied. "He says going to Idaho and live in Uncle Glenn's cabin for a while to sort things out and decide what to do next."

"There's nothing wrong with that," Maude said. "It sounds sort of nice and he needs a break. He should have done it a long time ago."

"The cabin is more of a shack," Marta said. "It's on a small lake—Trial or Trail or something like that. It's one room with a log stove and a loft with a bed in it. It might be good for a week's vacation, but nobody in his right mind would think of living there."

"Then he'll come back," Connie said with a shrug. "He can always find another apartment when he gets back."

They nodded and thought their own thoughts.

"What did you find at the house?" Susan asked, breaking the silence.

"A lot of dust," Maude laughed. "Libby would have more than two cents' worth to say about the way it looks right now. I knew he was having trouble keeping things together when he wasn't teaching. But I had no idea he'd been sleeping on the couch in the living room since she left. Their bed is made up and dusty and the living room looks like a cyclone went through."

"Randall was over there a lot at first," Marta said. "He had marching orders from Mom to check on Tanner. But even he didn't know how bad it's gotten."

"The guys are going to start on Thursday," Maude said. "I guess Tanner has them taking the furniture to a consignment shop. The store will take the posters and bigger furnishings, too. The little stuff we need to box for the Goodwill."

"We thought we'd take Wednesday to sort through things and claim anything we can use at BB's," Connie said to Susan. "Libby would like that."

"Someone needs to go through the office, too," Maude said. "I know the cops took a lot when they searched the house, but we should see what's left. She showed me some sketches of flyers she was working on for BB's, and I know she kept a file with notes on ideas for the place. You should have those if they're still there."

"I'll do that," Connie said.

"Do you think Tanner would care if we claimed the wing chairs for Bertram's library?" Susan asked. "There are four of them, I think. Those with the throw rug and the table in the office will make a cozy reading corner for the kids."

"He said to take whatever we want," Maude shrugged. "He just wants the place empty and clean so he can sell it."

"Can everyone be there at lunchtime on Wednesday?" Marta asked. "I'll bring what we got today. And I'll get more boxes before I come."

"No kids," Connie put in. "That would be more than we can handle."

The women nodded. The conversation stopped while they sipped their tea.

"Does anybody have any idea why she did this?" Maude asked. "Can you guess where she went?"

"I can guess why," Susan said without hesitation.

"Me, too," Connie said. "But I have no idea where."

"The Bertram House was her baby," Susan explained. "A lot of what's good about the place is good because of Libby's work. She kept coming up with ways to make it better."

"And she loved the kids," Connie put in. "She had a way with them. She could break the shell on even the hardest, most toughened kids we got."

"And that's the why of it," Susan continued. "Almost a year before she disappeared, Libby told me that it was getting harder and harder to make sure the kids got what was best for them. She said she thought there was a basic change in the court findings and the kids were getting the short end of the stick."

"Right," Connie cut in. "She told me the heart had gone out of the system. Her two cents' worth was that everything was done for expediency and not for the kids."

Susan nodded in agreement. The room was quiet while they all thought about Libby and how good she was with their children.

"Who were the kids she took?" Marta asked.

"Why were those kids so special?" Maude asked at the same time.

"They were left on Saint Augustine's steps one night," Susan explained. "A four-year-old boy and his twin sisters. The girls were two, I think. A cleaning crew found them when they came to work at midnight or something like that."

"Libby was furious that anyone would do that," Connie said. "She tried to get assigned to the case, but Sam was smart enough to see there would be trouble if she went to court with them. She was too attached and too angry to handle things objectively. So he recommended someone else, and the judge went with his recommendation."

"She spent a lot of time with them at BB's, though," Susan continued. "I guess everyone at Bertram's did. Even the older kids took a shine to them. They were the sweetest kids."

"Libby went to their hearing," Susan continued. "She told me the judge neglected to order them placed together. I think it was the last straw."

"I don't understand," Marta said. "What does that mean?"

Connie sighed.

"Well, Libby said that if the judge's order states the kids should be placed together, it pretty much assures that they'll stay together wherever they go," she explained. "But if that wording isn't there, they may or may not stay together. More likely, each one will go to a different foster home and then into the system where they get adopted into different families. It's hard to place siblings together, but with two it sometimes happens."

"With three it's almost impossible," Susan said. "I think when Libby heard the order she knew they'd be placed separately."

"So she took them and ran," Maude said, shaking her head.

"Yup," Connie and Susan said together.

"But I have no idea where she went," Connie said.

"Me either," Susan said.

After a quiet moment, Maude stood up.

"I hear little voices," she said. "I guess I'll go home and get supper started."

"Me, too," Marta said. "We're on for Wednesday, right?"

By spring, I'd sold the house and put my profit in a money market account. After Libby's postcards pushed me into action, family and friends rallied to help clean up the house and yard and get rid of all the things I wouldn't need in my future. That was nearly everything I owned. It was certainly all the stuff Libby had left behind. Whoever bought the house would get her well-cared-for garden tools, but I was getting rid of everything else. No pots, no bags of soil or weed killer, no seeds she collected and labeled, and no canning jars waiting to be filled.

Libby's women friends claimed some of the furniture for The Bertram House. They invited me to come and see the reading corner they'd set up in the library, but I couldn't bear it and said no thanks. The rest of the furniture went to a consignment shop. Without telling him, I set it up for the money to go to Uncle Glenn. He probably didn't need it, but I wanted to say thanks for being a friend all my growing up years.

I was sure shoppers at the local Goodwill would be very happy with the great things they'd find. I wasn't keeping anything Libby used to make our house a home and donating them was an easy way to get rid of them.

But as Dad said, I was moving on to Phase Four of my life, and I didn't need to take much with me. Phase One had been growing up in my parents' house, learning about being human, and figuring out how to make a living. Phase Two was the years between leaving their house and meeting Ms. Elizabeth Lindt. Phase Three was this house and the few years I'd shared it with Libby. Phase Four would be the rest of my life. I hoped I'd share it with Libby and the kids, but maybe not if I couldn't find them.

The last thing I did before I drove away from the house was paint the screw holes in the front door with the glossy blue paint Libby had left in the basement. I had the last dragon wrapped in a t-shirt in my duffle bag. I thought it was sad that no one else would ever know that three dragons once graced the door. It looked empty without them.

Once the house was cleaned out and the yard made presentable, I found a furnished apartment close to the academy. I decided to stop sleeping in the dorm so I wouldn't be tempted to answer questions about Libby or what I was going to do after retirement. I worked as many hours as I could, even teaching classes from other instructors' outlines and notes when they wanted time off. I saved every penny I could. For the first time in my life, I started accumulating cash and hiding it in my apartment. As a cop, I knew any self-respecting burglar could find my stashes, but I hid it away just the same.

As my self-imposed retirement date approached, I got a passport. I told everyone who was interested in my plans about my uncle's cabin in Idaho and the great fly fishing I'd be doing out there for a few months after I finished at the academy. I talked about a trip to Canada to check on the fishing in a lake so far from civilization that you had to fly in and didn't have cell phone reception. I talked about spending a season in Alaska.

Two weeks after the ceremony awarding me an engraved watch, I emptied the refrigerator and cleaned every nook and cranny of the apartment. Then I rented a motel room.

My last week was spent saying goodbye to my family and friends. They didn't know we were saying goodbye, but I tried to be certain each of them knew I loved them.

Dad and Uncle Glenn were easy. We spent one night at the tavern playing pool and swapping stories. For the first time in my life I saw them as brothers who were best friends. I envied the love they shared. I wouldn't have that now that I was leaving both Randy and Bill behind. By the time I dropped them back at the house, they were full of beer and content with their lives. They were obviously proud that they'd set me straight and got me moving on with my own life.

Mom was harder, but since it was spring I offered to go with her to find bedding plants for the yard. We shopped, had lunch, and I'm sure she knew how much I loved her when I helped unload the plants onto their porch.

Marta fed me in the kitchen of the big house where she was raising her kids. I spent hours that afternoon playing *Remember the time?* with her. Our conversation was interrupted again and again by her kids. I relished every one of those interruptions. She asked me back the next week, and I accepted.

Bill and Maude's dinner invitations had been declined so often since Libby left that I'm sure they were surprised when I accepted. After an excellent roast followed by lemon sorbet, Bill and I wrestled their three boys until it was time to put them to bed.

"Idaho," he said. We were standing on their porch waiting for Maude to get the kids to bed so I could say goodnight to her. "Why Idaho?"

"No reason except that's where Uncle Glenn's cabin is and I have a place to stay," I replied. "It's temporary. I just need a place to think about things and decide what to do next."

"But Idaho," Bill said as Maude joined us.

He put his arm around her and pulled her close. My heart squeezed tight. I knew I had to get away from them or I'd tell them what I was really doing. It had always been hard for me to keep a secret from Bill. And whenever I saw Maude, I remembered what a good friend she'd been to Libby.

"There are skinheads in Idaho," Bill said. "With your luck, you'll end up in trouble."

"Not this time," I tried to laugh. "I'm not taking Farley with me, so everything should be okay out there."

Bill and Maude laughed. They knew my Farley saga.

"Well, keep us posted," Maude said. "If you aren't back by August, I have the feeling someone on this porch will be joining you. If I know him, he'll probably bring three other men who are related to you to find out what's going on."

I laughed, hugged them, and went to my truck.

Only Randy was suspicious.

"What's going on, man?" he asked more than once the Saturday we took his son to the demolition derby. "You hate this."

"I do," I said. "But I figured I could sit through it just once to make you happy."

"Right," he said. "And pigs can fly."

We yelled over the motors and talked, talked and yelled, and finished the day off with burgers the size of dinner plates. Since it was probably the last one I'd have for a long time, I thought I might as well splurge. When we got back to their house, Randall sent my nephew inside and settled back in his seat.

"So what are you up to," he asked. "This is not like you."

"I'm not up to anything," I replied. "Can't I spend time with you without you getting suspicious?"

"No," Randall said. "We haven't spent time like this since...well, it's been so long that I can't really remember when. Maybe before I got married. And don't tell me about the times I came over after Libby left. They don't count because Mom sent me."

"Hmmm," I replied. We sat in silence for a bit.

"Okay," he said suddenly as he opened his door. "I guess we've had our fix. I'll bet we don't do this again until we both have gray hair. 'night."

"'night," I said. I watched him walk to his front door. He turned and waved. I felt the sting of tears as I drove away.

Sunday morning, I packed my duffle with the few things I was keeping, cushioning the dragon with clothes. I emptied my cash into a backpack and put a couple of shirts on top of that. I drove to the bus station, got a locker, and locked up the duffle and the backpack. Then I called a cab and sent them to my parents' address. In the truck, I signed the back of the title. I put it, along with the note I'd written the night before, in plain sight on the passenger's seat.

I parked the truck in the driveway where I knew Mom and Dad would see it when they got back from church. I wondered how long it would take for them to come out and look inside. They'd think I'd gone to the store or for a walk. Then they'd check my old room to see if I was asleep. They'd probably call Randall and Marta so see if they'd heard from me. Finally they'd get Uncle Glenn and he'd have them check the truck.

They'd find my note: *Give the truck to Randy's son when he's old enough to drive, here's the signed title. I think I've figured out where Libby is and I'm going to her. I probably won't be back. I don't know how to let you know I'm okay without giving her up. I love all of you but I won't give Libby up.*

The cab pulled in behind me and I had him take me back to the bus station. I bought a ticket to Boise, Idaho.

The duffle and backpack are caked with dust. My last shower was three days ago at a house renting rooms to down-and-out Americans in Hermosilla. My room hadn't locked, so I took everything with me to the bathroom down the hall. I stripped, put my dirty clothes in a plastic bag, and showered with the new bar of soap I'd packed in a blue plastic box made just for soap. Then I put on clean clothes and carried everything back to my room.

Last night I gave the maid a big tip to bring dinner to my room, and I ate standing up watching the street outside my window. Then I lay on the hard bed with the thin pillow folded under my head and looked at Libby's handwriting on the postcards. *My Two Cents.*

I'm taking a chance coming here, but I'm sure I'm right about what Libby meant with the postcards and the pennies. Her words on the cards are telling me she brought the kids here to keep them from being separated. The pennies meant her two cents' worth was that the court's decision wasn't good enough. She was taking justice into her own hands so the kids would have a better life. She was raising them, on her own, in a different country where the authorities hopefully didn't care whether or not she was their mother.

There was no other reason for those postcards with those specific words written on them to be left for me to find and figure out. The words and the shiny pennies would have made me think of this sooner if I'd been in any shape to go through the house myself. Instead I'd gotten so deep into self-pity that I hadn't even gone into our bedroom for eighteen months.

Libby couldn't have guessed it would take me so long to find the postcards. She must think I'm not coming. By now, she must have figured out how to live alone and raise the kids without me. I stare into the darkness until I fall asleep with the cards on my chest.

I sleep too long. I wake with a headache arching over the top of my head and into my eyes. I start with the first Advil of the day. I'll take many more before it's over. The Mexican sun is already high in the sky when I carry my duffle and backpack into the street and look around. I find breakfast and strong coffee, hoping the caffeine will help with the headache.

I talk with taxi driver after taxi driver until I find one willing to take me over the mountains. The man drives a hard bargain. He'll take me to Chihuahua for his usual rate, but I have to get packed lunches, buy all his gas, and promise to get him a room where he can sleep before he heads back. I agree to everything and go off to find our lunch while he fuels the car.

Hours after we leave Hermosilla we're still on the road in the hot sun. The trip seems much slower than the one I remember with Bill and Maude. And the road seems much rougher. But maybe it's just the same as it was. Maybe when I was with Bill and Maude I didn't care what was at the end of the road. Now I do.

The yellow VW Beetle with its taxi sign is a funny sight as it makes its slow progress up the mountain. We stop time and again to let the engine cool. The trunk is filled with bottles of warm water that go into us and into the car in unequal portions. Each time we stop, we eat from the food I brought and sit in whatever shade we can find. I speak very little Spanish and the driver speaks little English, so we communicate what we need to with gestures and sentences I construct using my Spanish-English dictionary. He laughs each time I pat my pockets, but I have to reassure myself that the postcards and the money I took from the backpack are still there every time we stop.

I buy several cans of cold pop and a burrito for each of us at a taco truck parked near the second gas station where we stop for fuel. After that, the road gets even steeper and I wonder if the old yellow Beetle is going to make it.

The road finally levels out and we pull into Chihuahua. Our first stop is a gas station where he once again fills the tank. The second is a motel where the driver signs in and I pay for his room. Then we walk down the street to a café, me still carrying the duffle and backpack. As we drink cold beer and wait for our food, I take a picture of Libby from my pocket and hand it to him.

"Can you ask the waiter if he knows this woman," I say, using the dictionary. I doubt the waiter will recognize Libby. Chihuahua seems like a small town to me, but it's probably bigger than I realize. Besides, she's just another American.

The cab driver looks at the picture and grins.

"Your woman?" he asks in English.

"Yes," I reply. I smile a weak smile. "I think she's here someplace."

He nods. I'm not sure he understands the words, but he understands the meaning. He holds up the picture when the waiter returns with plates heaped with food. The two of them have a rapid-fire conversation I can't follow. The waiter points his finger this way and that before grinning at me and going back to the kitchen. The taxi driver hands Libby's photograph back to me with a grin and a wave at my plate. Then he starts his meal.

We empty our plates, and I order another beer for each of us. When the beer comes, I get out my dictionary. I want to ask if the waiter recognized Libby. But before I can find any of the words I need, the driver waves his hand at the dictionary.

"I know," he says. "She is here."

There are questions I want to ask, but I can tell he has no patience left for me and my dictionary. We drink our beer, and when the bottles are empty I order two more. We sit in silence until the afternoon cools into evening. The café empties and then fills again. Finally the driver stands up and hefts my duffle over his shoulder. I pay our tab and follow him back down the street to the taxi.

He drives the narrow streets as if he knows where he's going. When he stops in front of a Catholic Church I can see the large copper nails holding together the huge wooden doors filling an arched doorway. I give him a quizzical look and he grins back at me.

"She is here," he says.

He gets out of the car, puts my duffle over his shoulder, and starts down the street. I follow him carrying my backpack. When we turn a corner, I can see why he parked the car. The street is no longer a street. It's a worn brick path between stucco walls of many different colors. He stops in front of a house with a blue door.

"She is here," he says and points.

He gives me a smile as he hands me the duffle. Then he turns and starts back to the taxi.

"Wait," I say to his retreating back. "Wait until I see if she's here."

"Your woman," he says, turning and walking backward to smile at me. "She is here."

I let him go. I paid for his motel room. If I need to, I know where to find him in the next few hours. I turn back to the blue door. Two familiar dragons spit their forked tongues at me. There's space for one more between them, and I he is in my bag. There is no doubt who lives here. I go cold. I swallow. The weight on my chest is painful.

The small house is bright yellow. There are long narrow windows next to the door and along the walls. Clumps of cactus are planted beside the short path between the street and the door. I drop the duffle and backpack and take in a deep breath.

I'm working up my nerve to use one of the dragons when faces peek from behind a curtain. Two tow-headed girls watch me for a minute and then disappear into the darkness of the house. I hear them running away as I lift a dragon tail and rap it down. The sound echoes through the house and goes quiet.

Nothing happens. No one comes. I use the dragon tail again and wait. Slowly, the door opens a few inches. A blonde-headed boy looks up at me cautiously. Then he pushes the door open a little further and the two girls, who look just like him, appear at his side.

"Hello," I say. I wonder if I should bend over or crouch down to their level. I do neither. "I'm looking for Libby."

The children watch me in silence for a minute. Then the two girls turn and, giggling happily, disappear into the house at a run. The boy reaches out and takes my hand. I pick up my things and let him pull me inside.

The house is cool and smells like spice. A half-wall topped with houseplants separates the small foyer from a room sparsely furnished with a couch, chair, and table. The wall I can see is filled with photographs of the children, of Libby, and of me. There are pictures of me with my parents, with Bill, in my uniform the day I graduated from the academy, at a birthday party with my siblings as I blow out my candles, and with Libby in front of our own blue door. The boy grins at me and points at the pictures. I wonder how and when Libby took these from our albums. I know why I never noticed they were gone.

I hear a door open and close. I hear excited little voices saying, "He's here! He's here! Dad is here!"

I take two steps further into the coolness as the little girls skip back to their brother. He lets go of me to put a hand on each of their shoulders. I can see why Libby fell in love with them. They have mischievous blue eyes with long lashes. Their round cheeks dimple with happy smiles. I see a protectiveness in the boy that seems perfectly natural even though he's so young. I feel the same emotion rising in me though this is the first time I've seen Libby's kids.

I look up at a sound in the back of the room. Libby stands in the doorway wearing one of my shirts. She is thinner than when I last saw her. She's carrying a basket filled with squash and tomatoes. She's tanned and her wild hair is loose around her face. My groin tightens as I remember my hands in that hair when it was wet and straight in the shower. My heart tightens when she smiles at the scene in front of her. The weight on my chest floats away and my eyes fill with tears.

"Hey," I say. That one word says everything I'm feeling.

Libby understands. She puts the basket on the table and tries to smooth her hair.

"You came," she says quietly.

"Took me a while," I reply. "I'll tell you all about it."

In two steps, she's in my arms. Her face presses against my chest and she laughs. She laughs that laugh as her arms go around me and her hair tickles my chin. I feel the vibration of it from my head to toes. My heart melts. The girls are hopping up and down around us in a happy dance. It feels like a dozen little hands are patting my legs. I put a hand on the boy's head and smile down at him over Libby's shoulder.

Then my face and hands are lost in Libby's wild hair. Three kids I don't know tug at my clothes, and I laugh. I laugh like I haven't laughed in years. I'm home. I can't believe it, but I'm home.

Made in the USA
San Bernardino, CA
21 August 2014